My Head Master

Published Works

Adamu Kyuka Usman   Hope in Anarchy
Adamu Kyuka Usman   The Lord Mammon
Adamu Kyuka Usman   The Butcher's Wife
Adamu Kyuka Usman   The Death of Eternity
Adamu Kyuka Usman   The Village Tradesman

My Head Master

By

Kyuka Lilymjok

Malthouse Press Limited

Lagos, Benin, Ibadan, Jos,Port-Harcourt, Zaria

© Kyuka Lilymjok 2017
First Published 2017
ISBN: 978-978-54775-7-3

Published and manufactured in Nigeria by

Malthouse Press Limited
43 Onitana Street, Off Stadium Hotel Road,
Off Western Avenue, Lagos Mainland
E-mail: malthouse_press@yahoo.com
malthouselagos@gmail.com
Website: malthouselagos.com
Tel: +234 802 600 3203

Dedication

To my wife Maria and my children: Justice, Sunfair, and
Fairprinces.

Those who inspire others,
Inspire their own immortality
Those who shape others
Shape their own destiny.

Table of Contents

Dedication

Chapters

1. A Man and his Manners - **1**
2. A Gleaming Roof and a Leaping Heart - **9**
3. The Damn Motorcycle - **16**
4. The Voice of Aboi-Abyin - **24**
5. Little Fingers, Little Ears - **30**
6. The Hawk, the Chick and the Vulture - **33**
7. The Missing Number - **41**
8. To Every Teacher his Due - **47**
9. Eyes in the House - **59**
10. Assembly and the Morning Dew - **58**
11. The Timekeeper and his Bell - **63**
12. Show me your Teeth - **70**
13. The Old Woman that would not Die - **76**
14. The Dust Exercise Book - **82**
15. Big Heads, Big Stomachs, Stupid Heads - **86**
16. The Vernacular Rule - **91**
17. The Visit of the School Inspector - **97**
18. Tyrant of the Football Field - **102**
19. Yashim, what is your Name? - **107**
20. A Recipe for Anomie - **113**
21. The Underbelly of an Angel - **121**
22. Jokes and our Little Skulls - **135**
23. The Trip to Zonkwa - **139**
24. The Last Supper - **148**

Chapter One

A Man and his Manners

I first saw the man who became my headmaster when he was riding his motorcycle past our house in Tyosa. He was a huge, dark, hairy man with big eyeballs that looked like they could see through anything and often saw through everything. His eyes were so frightening to me that I always trembled whenever he turned them on me. Not only were the eyeballs big, he had a way of baring them in the most frightening manner when he focused them on you. Older people said his father Akut was nicknamed *Akut the owner of frightening eyes* because of the largeness of his eyeballs. His eyeballs were said to be so big as to scare away birds whenever he entered the forest. Some people said they scared away chickens. So he was called *Akut the owner of frightening eyes.* But Akut's son was headmaster and no one dared pass his nickname to his son though he had passed his frightening eyes to the son. No one dared sing songs behind him the way children used to sing behind Akut his father.

The curl of his lips gave him the appearance of a severe man, and as I later came to find out, he was indeed a very severe man. My headmaster looked like a man with a lot of energy in him and I later found out he had a lot of energy in him. You could even sense this energy in the way he sat on his motorcycle. His two hands gripped the handles of the motorcycle very tightly, so tightly the veins at the back of his hands bulged out. His neck, which looked like the trunk of a python that had just swallowed something big, seemed also to bulge with his hands.

My headmaster liked hunting. He was to be found more in the forest after school than in his house. Antelopes and guinea fowls

1

were mostly the games he hunted. He hunted guinea fowls with traps and antelopes with his Dane gun. If he was going to hunt antelopes, his Dane gun strapped on his left shoulder, according to the gallops or smoothness of the path, swung violently or slightly about him as he rode his motorcycle. But if he only wanted to go and set or inspect his guinea fowl traps, he went to the forest without his gun. He hunted mostly in the forest after our village and that was why he was always on the path between Sarai and Tyosa.

My headmaster was the only person in Sarai and the surrounding villages that owned a motorcycle. Indeed, people who owned bicycles then in Sarai and the surrounding villages could be counted on the fingers of one hand. So my headmaster was always about the only motorist on the small path between Tyosa and Sarai. Even with this, he was never relaxed. He rode his motorcycle with about the same care and concentration as a motorist on a busy city highway. No one waved at him on his motorcycle and he waved back. No one greeted him and he greeted back – though in the case of the latter, it was foolish to greet my headmaster while he was on his motorcycle. The noise of the old Honda Benly was as deafening as that of a sawing machine.

Perhaps because of the intensity of his concentration while riding his motorcycle, he was always sweating in hot or cold weather. Trickles of sweat started from his forehead and ran down his massive chest down to the base of his torso soaking his dress. Sometimes, the sweat on his face got so much as to interfere with his vision. When asked why he was attending so much to his ride, he would say, 'the pigs; the damn pigs, the stupid pigs, the horrible pigs; those filthy creatures of hell you know. How I hate the filthy things. They would just stray into your path and… bang! One would think they have ears and could hear the sound of an approaching motorcycle, but no. Their unnerving snorts would not allow them hear anything. "Good, good, good," the pig keeps snorting, yet everything about the pig is bad. Always looking for food, their yawning stomachs had nailed their ears against all thoughts of danger.'

That was one thing about my headmaster – long speech. A simple question that could be answered in one sentence, my headmaster would go into some sort of lecture. The villagers always stood in need of education and he was the one to give it.

On the day I first saw him, after he rode past me on his motorcycle, he stopped by Baushe who was working in his farm beside the path. Although Baushe and my headmaster could not be described as friends, Baushe was the only person in Tyosa my headmaster often stopped his motorcycle to exchange pleasantries with. Baushe went to a pastors' training school, but could not finish because he put the daughter of one of his teachers in the family way and was sent packing from school. People said instead of Baushe returning to the village with a certificate, he returned with a pregnant woman, both carrying shame on their heads like bundles of firewood. As someone with some knowledge of the Bible, Baushe was made an elder in the church despite his sin of fornication.

'Knowledge is good,' I heard Baushe saying to my headmaster.

'Knowledge is a hill,' said my headmaster. 'Ignorance is a hole. Knowledge is a throw, ignorance is a fall. Knowledge is a push, ignorance is a pull.'

'If only I can acquire more knowledge…' Baushe began, allowing the remaining of what he wanted to say to hang on the frame of his frustration.

'Yes, knowledge is progress,' said my headmaster, waving his hand about like a flaying machete. 'But the way forward may not always lead to heaven. It may lead to hell. Heaven may be where you are, where ignorance like elephantiasis of the scrotum is determined to keep you.'

Anyone who knew Baushe's circumstances and did not know my headmaster might think he said this to mock or console Baushe. But nothing would be farther from my headmaster's intention. My headmaster was a man of opposing views. What he had just said were his opposing views on knowledge and ignorance.

'If only I can acquire more knowledge,' Baushe said, dreamingly. There was nothing in his voice or face to show he heard what my headmaster said.

'No doubt knowledge heals and ignorance sickens,' said my headmaster. 'But ignorance sometimes is a better friend than knowledge. We will one day find out that if we knew all the facts about life, we wouldn't have been able to live it. If people know when they will die, you can imagine what they will do. What the mind does not know the heart does not grieve over and you know life is in the heart. There is blissful ignorance, but no blissful knowledge because I think knowledge always brings pain. There is nothing as good to health as the mind feeding the heart with happiness instead of pain. There are some ways in which darkness is better than light, you know.'

My headmaster always spoke loudly. When asked why he was always talking loudly even to someone standing before him, he would say, 'how do you blame me? 'People are becoming deaf and you have to shout. I really don't know what is the cause of their deafness and I don't think they know themselves. But even the sheep knows people are deaf. So you have to shout to be heard nowadays. We should pray that very soon we don't have to scream. If people cannot hear you because you are speaking so inaudibly, you will be speaking to yourself and that is madness. Now madness you know can be a very embarrassing thing, not to the mad man though, but to others – particularly those unfortunate to be his relations. Before I came to be headmaster in Sarai, I was in Takako. There was this man Katunku who walked and talked alone. No one heard what he mumbled as he walked and spoke alone, but everyone could see the movement of his lips and those with keen ears could even hear the guttural sounds coming from his lips. Because no one heard him, everyone said he was mad. He confirmed what people were saying when he started pointing at trees in a threatening manner as he spoke alone in the bush. His madness became a settled matter when he went beyond threatening trees with his fingers to attacking them. He would slap a tree with his open palm and begin to wrestle with it. Do you know why Katunku went mad? He was taking too many herbs and some of the herbs affected his brain and his mind was turned upside down.'

A mad man is called *abwak-apyia* in Tyap which literally means one whose head is about-turned. As a child, when I heard my parents refer to somebody as *abwak-apyia,* I expected to see the man with an about-face – someone with his face facing his back and the back of his head facing his front. It was only when my headmaster started talking of a mad man as someone whose mind was turned upside down that I began to understand what madness was all about.

My headmaster hated pigs so much that I was not surprised when I learned he did not eat pork. Pigs he would say are creatures of hell always with their snouts to the ground pleading with *Aboi-abyin* the spirits of the ancestors and the gods of the earth to give them food and to have mercy on them. If by mercy they meant the butcher's knife be held off their throats for a while, there was no doubt they were creatures, which stood in need of mercy with the disconcerting noise coming from their noses. But they won't get any mercy from my headmaster. He would sooner slay all the pigs in Sarai and the surrounding villages and leave them for the vultures, which he called their cousins in the air, than give them a hearing.

Whenever my headmaster was riding his motorcycle, he had his helmet on. It was a yellow helmet frequent and long use had almost turned grey. The strap that passed over his chin to hold the helmet firmly on his head had come off from each side it was screwed. My headmaster had improvised another strap that bore little resemblance with the one that came with the helmet. While the original strap was dark and ligature-like, the one my headmaster improvised was green and a little too wide. To fit the new strap into the helmet, he bored a little hole on each point the original strap was screwed. He knotted the strap permanently on the left side of his head leaving the other side to hang loose. Whenever he put on the helmet, he knotted the loose end of the strap on his chin after passing it through the little hole he bored on the other side of the helmet.

The thumb of the left hand of my headmaster was never far from the horn of the motorcycle. To some people, the noise of the Honda Benly was enough to warn people of his approach without adding the horn to it. But my headmaster thought differently. Amidst the din of noise generated by the engine of the old motorcycle, a more definite sound that set itself apart as the horn of the motorcycle would rise above the noise of the engine to tell people that my headmaster was coming. Let every pig keeps its snout out of the path.

On the day I saw my headmaster for the first time, before he finished his discussion with Baushe, I ran back home where my father was working in our farm to know from my father who my headmaster was.

My father told me he was the headmaster of the primary school at Sarai.

'He is on a motorcycle,' I said, panting with excitement.

'It is his motorcycle,' said my father.

'When I grow up, I will buy a motorcycle,' I said with a lot of feelings.

'When you grow up and have money,' said my father with a metallic edge to his voice.

'When I grow up and have money,' I repeated what my father had said without its meaning sinking into my mind. It was only when my mother repeated the same statement days after that its meaning sank into my mind.

'It is good to own a motorcycle,' I murmured, dreamingly.

'Yes,' said my father. 'But for you to own a motorcycle, you must be a headmaster. If you are a headmaster, a motorcycle is nothing to you. You can buy a lorry if you like. You can even buy an aeroplane. A headmaster is not a small man. He is a big man with a lot of money.'

'How does he get the money?' I asked, fascinated by what my father had said.

'From his office,' said my father. 'In his school there are many pupils and teachers. Any money the government sends to the school to buy books for the pupils or to take care of the teachers passes through his hands. In addition, the government pays him a big salary every month.'

'Father, I will like to be a headmaster,' I said, enchanted by what my father was saying.

'That will be good,' said my father. 'But you must go to primary school first and be good in what you are taught. When you come out of primary school with a good result, you will then go to college. It is after your college education that you can become a headmaster.'

'Father, when will I enrol in primary school?'

'You are not yet of age, my child. When you are, I will take you to the primary school at Sarai. But one of these days I will take you to a little hill near Chok stream for you to have a glimpse of the roof of the primary school.'

Two days after I first saw him, my headmaster returned to our village in the rain. He was wearing a raincoat and rain boots. I wondered where his motorcycle was. Later I learned he could not ride the motorcycle to our village because the little bridge over Chok stream had been washed away by a flood, which was still raging when my headmaster came to the stream. The stream being very close to our village, my headmaster decided to leave his motorcycle there and trek to the village.

For a long time I kept dreaming of owning a raincoat and rain boots. I would tell my mother that when I grow up, I will buy raincoat and rain boots and I will walk majestically with them around our village the way I saw my headmaster walking around with his.

'When you grow up and have money,' said my mother. 'There are many grown ups who don't have money and cannot buy rain boots and raincoats. In this neighbourhood who beside the headmaster have you seen with raincoats and rain boots? Is he the only grown up in the neighbourhood?'

It was now I understood what my father told me earlier. Growing up does not necessarily mean having money. With me before now, growing up was synonymous with having money. Thus I would say when I grow up, I will buy a bicycle, shoes and all other things I admired. But now that my father and mother had fostered this new awareness in me, I knew I had to become a headmaster to be able to afford these things I would like to own. This increased my love for school. For, like my father had said, I had to go to school to become a headmaster.

There was no primary school in my village Tyosa. The only primary school near our village was in Sarai where my headmaster was headmaster. Sarai was a village about four kilometres away from my village. Most of these four kilometres was forest land with a small river running through the forest. The river made the forest looked thicker than it would have been. Before my father said the roof of the school could be seen from a hill near Chok stream, I never knew it could.

Chapter Two

A Gleaming Roof and a Leaping Heart

A few days after I saw my headmaster, my father on my insistence, took me to the little hill where the roof of the primary school at Sarai could be seen. When we climbed the hill, I could see the zinc roof of the primary school gleaming in the sun. The moment I saw the gleaming and twinkling roof of the school, my heart leapt to it and never returned.

The primary school was the only building in Sarai and the surrounding villages with zinc roofing. All other buildings were roofed with thatch. But the primary school was not only roofed with zinc, it was plastered with cement and painted white. It was like a neon sign in a dark alley. All eyes were on it. In Tyosa, after my father showed me the roof of the school from the little hill, I used to go and stand on the little hill just to catch a glimpse of the roof, which was the only part of the building that I could see standing on the hill. Against the sun, the roof would be twinkling like a million stars marched into one. Though the stars were one, they were still separate. One star came on and another star went off in a most bewitching manner. Sometimes all the stars were on and flowed down the roof like little diamonds through the fingers of a diamond cutter after he is through with polishing his diamonds. When this happened, the stars turned into water towards the eaves of the roof only to emerge as stars once more at the top of the roof. The pastor of our church spoke of the lamp of Christ set upon a hill. When I grew older, I used to wonder if the school roof was some kind of lamp.

Whenever I stood on the little hill looking at the roof of the primary school, my mind often was not with me. It was always with the roof and what it represented to me. Standing on the little hill, my mind would be full of imaginations and fantasies of the many good things in the school. Often while standing on the little hill, I thought of being able to read and write; I thought of being able to own raincoats, rain-boots and other articles of refinement that going to school held the promise of and I was impatient to be enrolled as a pupil in the school.

I must say this now that even as a little child, I had a strong passion for learning and education and as I later came to find out, I had an intelligence quotient relatively higher than most children of my age in our village. In the rainy season which was the season of folktales – folktales were not told in the dry season which was the season for hunting out of fear that hunters would not be able to kill games when they went out to hunt, our grandmother used to tell us folktales. Once I was told a story, it stuck to my brain and I could tell it with about the same accuracy as our grandmother when even my older siblings would not remember important details of the story. Because of my keen interest in such tales, whenever meat was cooked in our house and our grandmother teased us that she would only tell her stories to the person who surrenders his meat to her, I was always the first child to say she could have my meat. At a very young age, I knew about the same folktales as our grandmother. I was so good at story telling that whenever our grandmother was not around, my siblings used to ask me to tell them one story or the other that we had been told together by our grandmother. Initially, I was too glad to tell such stories without a price. But when their demands increased, I started asking for meat or some other priced item from the person who wanted me to tell him a story. Unlike my grandmother, however, I would not be teasing anybody. I always meant to have the meat or whatever it was that I asked for and depending on the desperation of the person, I might have what I asked for or a taunt for being so shrewd and calculating. When I became enrolled in primary school, one day my half-brother much older than me and in a higher class than me came and called me to recite in a-story-telling hour in his class names of towns and villages which our father knew by heart and had recited to us many times at home. My half-brother had attempted reciting the names of the towns and villages, but got stuck midway. His classmates laughed and booed him. Suddenly he remembered I could recite the names accurately and he came for me. I obliged him after he promised to give me some of the mangoes I knew he had at home. When I finished reciting the names of the towns and villages in a sing-song, the pupils in my half-brother's class and even the teacher were full of admiration for me. But my performance only helped to hold up my half-brother among his classmates as an imbecile of sort. They started jeering and booing him again to the point that I took pity on him and told him outside his class that he could keep his mangoes.

The fascination the primary school held for me, it held for most other children of my age and even those older than us. It was I who took most of my age mates to the little hill to show them the gleaming roof. Like me, they also climbed the little hill to have a glimpse of the gleaming roof. Some of the big boys also used to climb the hill with us. One of them said the zinc was white because it was brought by a white man. He said our thatch, particularly when it was getting old, bore our colour. Below the roof, the big boys said they could also see the walls of the school, which were painted white and which they claimed were gleaming against the sun even more than the roof. We the younger ones believed them then. But when I grew up to their height, I knew they were lying because I could not while standing on the hill see the wall they claimed to be seeing. It was then I knew why they used to refuse carrying up any of us the little ones to also see the walls of the building they claimed to be seeing.

The school roof excited me more than anything in my village. Wanting to see more of it one day, I decided quite secretly to go to Sarai where the primary school was, not only to see the roof at a closer range, but the walls of the school that I could not see standing on the little hill at Tyosa.

This was against my father's warning when he took me to the little hill to have a glimpse of the roof of the school. My father had said to me in a very stern voice, 'That is the school you will one day attend. But if I hear that you went to the school on your own before your time, I will never enrol you in it and that means you will never become a headmaster.'

I told him I would not attempt going to the school and meant it then. But a few days after leaving the hill with him, the urge to go to the school was too great for me. Unknown to my father and everyone in our house, I sneaked to the school. So as not to be prevented from embarking on my trip, I allowed older children who were already attending the primary school to leave Tyosa for the school before I set out for the same destination. It was a long trek for a child of my age and one full of fear. As I walked, I could hear the footsteps of somebody walking behind me. But when I looked back, I would see nobody. Then I would no longer hear the sounds of the footsteps. However, when I turned to continue my journey, the sounds of the footsteps would return to my ears clearer than before. At a point, I could no longer bear it. So I turned to face where I was coming from and began to walk backwards towards my destination. Now there were no footsteps. But moving backwards proved a tricky and dangerous way of walking a small, meandering path like the one between Tyosa and Sarai. Several times, I walked off the path and fell over a shrub by the wayside. I nearly sustain a sprain in my right ankle when I collided with a tree and fell on my hands and knees. It was then I gave up my attempt to make it to Sarai by walking backwards. I started walking the normal way and the sound of the footsteps returned once more making my heart to thump wildly in fear.

My fear heightened as I drew near river Yatuk which lay between Sarai and Tyosa. Although not a big river, river Yatuk was full of big trees that gave it the appearance of a grove from whichever direction it was approached. It was from this river that *akrusak* the resurrected mystique from the land of the dead used to emerge before he was brought to dance in front of the *Aboi* shrine during *Ayet-Atyap* – the *Aboi* festival. The flute man who would bring out the mystique may make several trips to Musa's or Aje-eet's house playing his flute that in a mesmerizing tune said to everyone:

> *Krusak yat akaniah ma Musa*
> *Krusak yat akaniah ma Je-eet*
> *Owo wu wo wuu.*

The song meant that the mystique is the kinsman of Musa's house and Aje'et's house. This gave the impression the mystique would come out of any of these houses he was said to be a kinsman. The women dancing in the small forecourt before the shrine who had been led by the flute man to think the mystique would come out of either of these houses would also be singing:

> *Krusak yat akaniah ma Musa*
> *Krusak yat akaniah ma Je-eet*
> *Owo wu wo wuu.*

But often all the trips by the flute man to either of these houses were dummies he was selling to the people. In the end, it would be from river Yatuk *akrusak* would emerge from the land of the dead to entertain and mystify the living. Aje-eet was my paternal grandfather and so *akrusak* was my kinsman. But I was not an initiate of the Aboi-oracle. My father had converted to Christianity and had refused any of his children be initiated into the Aboi-oracle. Each *Aboi* festival we watched with awe as children whose fathers were yet to convert to Christianity were carried kicking and crying into the shrine of *Aboi-abyin* to be initiated into the ancestral oracle. No child initiated into the oracle ever came out of the *Aboi* shrine and remained the same. If he was a delinquent before his initiation, he became well behaved after his initiation and was likely to remain so throughout life. It was said what a child was shown inside the shrine was enough to reform anybody for a lifetime. Because of what a child went through in that shrine, some children without enduring power died in the shrine and were buried in the shrine by the ancestors. Those that survived the ordeal, to use the Christian language, became born again forever. Because of the fear of what a child suffered inside the shrine, we whose parents had converted to Christianity were always envied by those whose parents were yet to embrace the new faith. But we also envied those who had been initiated into the *Aboi-oracle*. We observed that *akrusak* always chased us more during the *Aboi* festival than he chased initiates, who after all were his followers.

Because I was a non-initiate, though *akrusak* was supposed to be my kinsman, my fear of the mystique like that of any child of my age that was a non-initiate, was a mortal one. Instead of being initiated into the Aboi-oracle, I was dreaming of being enrolled into the primary school at Sarai that had become the new shrine and the new Aboi-oracle. It was indeed that shrine I was now sneaking to, to perceive more of its wonders ahead of my initiation. While I would have been carried by force into the Aboi shrine to be initiated into the Aboi-oracle, I was stealing away from home to go and peer at the white man's shrine.

I was now inside river Yatuk. In the words of my people, my head, out of fear, rose up to embrace the sky. I bolted into a run out of the river and kept running towards Sarai and the primary school. Curiously, while running, I was not hearing the sound of any footsteps behind me any longer. So I kept running until I could run no more. When I was tired of running, I sat down to rest under a tree not far away from the path. The tree was in a farm of guinea corn that looked so luxuriant.

Already Sarai and the primary school were within sight. While I rested, I was thinking of what to do when I get to the school. I have to be careful no pupil from my village sees me at school to report back to my parents. As I sat thinking of what to do, I heard the sound of my headmaster's Honda Benly resonating through the bush I had just emerged from. I was shocked. My headmaster that I thought was at school was not there but was in fact following me behind to the school. Where could he have gone to? He certainly had not ridden his motorcycle through my village because I would have heard the blasting sound of the machine. Well, there was no time for me to keep wondering where my headmaster went because from the rising noise of the old Honda Benly, he would emerge from the forest any moment and find me standing under the tree and that could be a lot of trouble for me. Immediately I hid behind the tree I was resting under where I hoped he would not see me while riding past. If he sees me, I could be certain my father would know I disobeyed him and that meant I would not become a headmaster.

Chapter Three

The Damn Motorcycle

I remained crouched behind the tree waiting for my headmaster to ride past where I was hiding, but he did not appear. The sound of his motorcycle was drawing nearer, but he was yet to emerge from the forest into the clearing that surrounded Sarai where I was. Suddenly the sound of the motorcycle ceased. What could be the problem? I wondered. Had the motorcycle developed a fault or had my headmaster parked it and gone into the bush to ease himself? What was I to do now that my headmaster might not ride past me as fast as I had earlier thought? If I remained crouched behind the tree, I might have to be there for an inordinately long time that I could not afford. The owner of the farm where I was might turn up and think I was relieving my bowels in his farm and start trouble. I could still remember how Kulien threw a stone at Tokan thinking the latter was defecating in his farm when he was only cutting *shushock* leaves to roast millet pap. The rainy season was not a period people wanted to see anyone squatting in their farms because of the unsightly and nauseating faeces. But if I leave and continue with my journey to the school, my headmaster would definitely meet me on the path if his motorcycle had no fault but he had merely turned it off to relieve himself in the forest. I didn't want him to see me not knowing what that might lead to. I was so absorbed in my thoughts that I was not even looking in the direction my headmaster would eventually come from. So I did not see him coming up the path pushing his motorcycle until he was quite close to where I was; I would not say where I was hiding because thoughts of hiding were not as much in me then as thoughts of how to move on to the school without having to meet my headmaster. Now it was too late to move. My best hope was to remain as motionless as possible and allow my headmaster to move past me; then I would follow behind when he had gone far. I was lucky I was sufficiently screened from him by the guinea corn in the farm.

My headmaster was pushing his motorcycle with his two hands, holding the handles in about the same way he held them when he was riding. His helmet was not on his head but hanging on the left handle of the motorcycle. This was the first time I was seeing him without the helmet on his head and he looked odd to me. His head was bent low and his eyes glued to the path. Occasionally he looked up as if to scan the sky for rainclouds and then sideways as if to scan the bush that thronged the path. It was not a hot day, but he was sweating profusely. Even from where I was, I could see the sweat cascading down his fat face. When he drew closer to where I was, his eyes and even the drops of sweat that frequently hung from his eyebrows before falling off or before they were wiped away by him, seemed to be glaring at the motorcycle he was pushing. I could also hear faint guttural noises, seemly to his current state, coming from his nose and half-open mouth. He must be complaining about the motorcycle I thought. When he drew closer to me, I could hear him cursing the motorcycle. 'This damn motorcycle,' he kept swearing at the motorcycle. He was swearing in such a bitter tone that I thought at a point he might stop and find a whip to flog the motorcycle for being so heartless and wicked. He did not do that, but he was pushing the motorcycle in such a rough manner that he was not avoiding potholes or the roots of trees along the path. Rather he was pushing it against all obstacles on the path though he could avoid most of them. The rear mudguard which was hanging onto the motorcycle or which the motorcycle was hanging onto by cable wires passed through holes bored at the fringes of the mudguard and tied to the shock absorbers was rattling very loudly. In my ears, it was like the mudguard was squealing against its being held to the motorcycle which apparently needed the mudguard than the mudguard needed it. The helmet hanging on the left handle of the motorcycle was swinging back and forth with only my headmaster's left hand as its wedge. The motorcycle no doubt was receiving a flogging worse than the one I initially thought of. The helmet went on swinging back and forth between my headmaster's hand and the speedometer of the motorcycle. When he took off his hand to wipe off sweat from his forehead with a handkerchief I thought took more sweat to his forehead than remove the one that was there, the helmet fell off the motorcycle.

My headmaster stopped walking and first attempted to stand the motorcycle on its single stand. He straightened up to wipe away more sweat from his face some of which was entering his eyes and affecting his vision. The motorcycle hoisted on a single stand stood only for a while before the stand sank into loose soil and the motorcycle fell on the same side the helmet had fallen, indeed on the helmet. 'The damn motorcycle!' my headmaster swore, going to raise the motorcycle from the ground. 'I hope it has not damaged my helmet.' He raised the motorcycle and hoisted it on a double stand and on firmer ground. I could see the veins in his neck bulging out of his skin as he was heaving the motorcycle to place it on the double stand. After he had hoisted the motorcycle, he went and picked the helmet from the ground and started examining it for damage. He found the damage he feared the helmet had sustained on the inner lining of the helmet. One of the rear footrest of the motorcycle had ripped open the inside lining at the centre of the helmet leaving the helmet metal bare. For sometime, he held the helmet with his left hand with the helmet inside facing my direction. His eyes were on the motorcycle and from the expression on his face, his thoughts about it were unpleasant thoughts. After standing and looking at the motorcycle for what to me was an inordinately long time, he pushed off the motorcycle from the double stand and began walking again to the school. The helmet was now on his head. Perhaps he wanted to have a feel of it with the tear on. Perhaps he wanted to avoid another accident. I allowed him to move far away from me, then I left the tree where I had been and began walking towards the school also.

I got to the school during break-time and was surprised to see everyone outside playing. Boys were in the football field playing football while girls were in the basketball court playing basketball. Boys and girls were playing volleyball together in the volleyball court not far away from the basketball court and several other children were engaged in other games that could involve only the child engaged in the game or two children. I could see James who was from Tyosa playing football in the football field. I could also see Timbwak also from Tyosa playing volleyball. In the basketball court, I could see Esther among the girls playing that game. While I could see them, I took care no one saw me. Only a few pupils were walking around not involved in any sport. Was learning in school all about sports? I wondered, despairingly. If it were, one might as well have enough of it in our river where we used to go and play.

But my major disappointment came from the roof of the school which had always fascinated me from Tyosa. So near it now, the roof was not twinkling as it was from Tyosa. The lamp of Christ which sparkled in Tyosa was a dull flicker in Sarai where it was set. The walls of the school older children had claimed were gleaming more than the roof were not gleaming at all. To think I had taken all the trouble to come to the school only to meet this was very painful and distressful to me. As I stood looking at the school in disappointment, I felt someone nudging me from behind. I turned to find Zwahu laughing at me. Zwahu was my cousin whose meat I once claimed before I told him a folk story. For days, he had begged me to tell him the story of the hare and the hyena and I only consented when he agreed to surrender his meat to me. Now I was at his mercy. How he came so close to me without my hearing his footsteps, I did not know. He was laughing, but I could not

19

laugh. I was so afraid particularly of my father hearing what I had done that I could not think.

'What are you doing in school?' I heard Zwahu asking. That was the third time he was asking the same question without an answer from me and there was not going to be an answer to that question that not only struck fear into me, but I felt was mocking me.

'You came to see the secrets of the school walls, is that not it?' he asked, examining my face in the most probing way. 'You little children of nowadays want to know everything, ehn? That is why you should have been initiated into the Aboi-oracle where you would be taught how to keep secrets and how not to try to uncover secrets hidden from you. But your father is a Christian and there is nothing I can do about it. But it is bad. A small boy like you prying into things he should not pry into.'

'Please, Zwahu don't tell anyone I came to school,' I pleaded. In addition to my fear that I was found where I ought not to be found, I had always feared Zwahu's father. He was said to bite off the ears of naughty little children. So whenever he came to our house, all the children would start crying. Part of the fear I had for the father I had for the son.

'If you are looking for where to hide, the lion's den is not the proper place. Where you were hiding is my den.'

'I beg you. I don't want my father to know I came to school.'

'So you also beg.'

Even as a child, I knew something was coming.

'There is more to life than being able to tell a story.'

'Yes there is.'

'Things can be funny.'

'Yes they can.'

'You owe me some meat."

It was finally out. 'Yes I know.'

'When can I have it?'

'Whenever meat is cooked in our house.'

'How will I know that meat is being cooked in your house?'

'I will tell you.'

'I don't trust you.'

'Please, do.

'No, I can't. Trust is the faith of foolish people and I am wise. But if I must trust anyone on this our little understanding, I will rather trust Sankwai your elder brother to inform me of the happy event.'

Sankwai was my senior brother that I had twice claimed his meat to tell him a story. If Zwahu tells him what I had done, he might also blackmail me.

'You can ask him to tell you when there is meat in our house, but please, don't tell him what I had done.'

'I will not tell him.'

'Thank you.'

'That is not all,' he said.

I waited wondering what else he wanted from me.

'In addition to giving me your meat, you will now be telling me stories without my having to pay for them. If you don't, I will tell your father the story that you came to school. Besides you, there are other people that can tell stories.'

The bastard was trying to screw everything out of me and in the fear I was, I could not resist him. So I consented to this demand also.

Now that he had gotten what he wanted, I could see he was desperate I leave the school. If I were seen by more pupils from Tyosa, he would lose the hold he had on me. It was then I realized it would not be in his interest to tell Sankwai my brother that I had come to the school. Blackmail is a funny thing. It is only a useful weapon if the blackmailer is the only one with the negative information. The more people come to know of the negative thing, the more the blackmailer loses the terror he holds over his victim.

'Now you have to go,' he said, looking furtively around him. 'Somebody else might see you. That means more trouble for you.'

He spoke in such a tone and countenance that it might be thought it was so much for my own good that I should leave and nothing of his own account.

'Yes, I will leave,' I said, but not making to go.'

'Unless you leave, I will …'

The school bell rang to tell the pupils break-time was over. Zwahu ran off to his classroom without completing his sentence. Though he did not complete it, it sounded like another threat. On the little matter of my going to school without permission, he was becoming a serial blackmailer.

I remained where I was, relieved I no longer ran the risk of being seen by another pupil from my village since all the school pupils were running into their classes. Moments after all the pupils were in their classes, I saw my headmaster coming out of a room I later came to know as his office. The room was at the centre of the long building that was the primary school. He was holding a very big ruler in his right hand and a packet of chalk in the left. He walked to the classroom next to his office and entered it.

'Good morning, children,' I heard the booming voice of my headmaster coming from the classroom.' I knew 'Good morning' because my older siblings already attending school everyday filled my ears with, 'Good morning, Good afternoon, Good evening and Good night.'

'Good morning sir,' the pupils chorused.

The next thing I heard was:

This is Toma
This is Tani
Pick it up Toma
Pick it up Tani
Then I heard:
This is the house that Toma built.
This is the food that is in the house that Toma built.
This is the rat that eats the food that is in the house that Toma built.

This is the cat that eats the rat that eats the food that is in the house that Toma built.

This is the dog that chases the cat that eats the rat that eats the food that is in the house that Toma built.

This is the stick that beats the dog that chases the cat that eats the rat that eats the food that is in the house that Toma built.

This is the fire that burns the stick that beats the dog that chases the cat that eats the rat that eats the food that is in the house that Toma built.

This is the water that puts out the fire that burns the stick that beats the dog that chases the cat that eats the rat that eats the food that is in the house that Toma built.

All these were things I had heard my siblings attending the primary school singing at home. So I was familiar with them though I did not know what they meant. Though I did not know the meaning of the recitations, I was very excited hearing my headmaster reading and the pupils reading after him. I moved closer to the class to hear more of what my headmaster would teach his pupils. I heard him, but it was not something I was familiar with and it was also not recited by the pupils in a sing-song like *Toma and Tani* or *The house that Toma built.* Since I did not like what he was saying, I left the school and started walking home. Besides, with all the pupils in their classes, I was now the only person outside and I could easily attract the attention of any passerby. I left without realizing most of the expectations that took me to the school that morning. Instead, I was now the victim of blackmail of one who thought he should be as shrewd as I in exploiting situations. But it had not been all losses. I had listened to my headmaster teaching his pupils and it was so thrilling to me though I was yet to understand the English language he was using to teach the pupils. I left the school full of determination of getting enrolled in school so that I would be able to understand English, speak the language and become a headmaster like my headmaster.

Chapter Four

The Voice of Aboi-Abyin

'If ever I become a headmaster in my life,' I kept saying to myself as I walked from the primary school at Sarai back to Tyosa, 'I would be a very great man with severe attitudes like my headmaster. If I want to eat rice and beans – *boys and girls* as I heard pupils already attending the primary school called them, they will be there for me. If I want to drink tea, I can have my fill. Look at that school; the whole of it is under his authority. If he wants the roof taken off today, it will be taken off. If he wants a better roof to replace the one taken off, he will have it. If he wants more raincoats and rain boots, he would have them. Of all my headmaster's possessions, I desired his rain boots more than any other. Often I imagined I had them on and I would strut about majestically the way I saw my headmaster walking around with his.

My love for my headmaster's rain boots was not unconnected with my general love for shoes. I had a cousin who was living in Kaduna with his parents. At Christmas, he used to come to the village with shoes and newly sewed clothes. I had little love for his clothes, but I pined for his shoes. One Christmas when he came to the village, I begged him to give me his shoes to try on my feet. He did and the feel of the shoes on my feet which had not known even flip-flops was exhilarating. He literally had to force me to take his shoes off my feet. After I had taken the shoes off, he and I went off to our little playground full of sand. At the playground, he would stamp his shoes on his feet on the sand and he would step away from the impressions left by the shoes. I would move close to the shoes' impressions looking at them excitedly. As a child, I made shoes of leaves and other forest growths and wore them. As a child,

I used to say if ever I own shoes, I will never take them off my feet even when going to sleep.

Now going back home after leaving the school, my thoughts were on my headmaster's rain boots. If ever I am able to buy rain boots, I will never take them off my feet. There would be nothing more pleasurable to my feet than such boots. Thinking of my headmaster and his boots, I came to river Yatuk. My thoughts of my headmaster left me and my fear of the river returned. Footsteps I did not hear behind me before, I was now hearing. As soon as I entered the river, I heard the eerie cry of *Aboi-abyin*. My heart plunged down and I think I fainted out of fear, because I later found myself lying in the shallow water of the river.

Aboi-abyin – the spirits of our ancestors, were everywhere. As a child, when my grandfather who was the *Agwa-aboi* – the leader of the Aboi-worshippers, died, it was *Aboi-abyin* that announced his death to us. He was sick for many months. Two days before his death, he seemed to have recovered. The old man who could not talk before could now talk. But most of what he said was understood only after his death. On the evening of his death, he told my father they had come for him and he was going on a very long journey. At sunset, we saw smoke coming from the thatch of his room and the roof shaking violently as if it would fall off the building. Amidst the smoke and shaking of the roof, we heard the eerie and esoteric cry of *Aboi-abyin*. My grandfather had died and the ancestors were telling the living they had come to carry one of their own to the land of the dead. The same fear I had that time was the one I had now. In fact, I had more fear now being alone in a river as I was and knowing I had done what I ought not to have done. *Aboi-abyin* usually cried when one had committed an offence. If one went to the river to cut bamboo sticks which were cut only once in a year by the whole village on a day appointed by the village-keeper, *Aboi-abyin* would cry out against the offender. If someone stole another's garden egg or some other crop, *Aboi-abyin* would cry out against the offender. When *Aboi-abyin* cried out against you, you would be sick and might even die if the ancestors were very angry at what you had done and they were not appeased.

I had no doubt *Aboi-abyin* was now crying against me because I had gone to school when my father had forbidden me.

But my father is a Christian I thought. *Aboi-abyin* cannot touch me. My father had taught us that whenever we heard the cry of *Aboi-abyin* we should say, '*Aboi-abyin* the ears of the ground, the eyes of the waters and the mouth of the trees; take care of your own and let Christ take care of his own. Your share and those who follow you is in the ground where you are and mine is in heaven where Christ is.' That when we say this, we would no longer hear the eerie, frightful cry of the ancestors. What our father taught us had long become a memory verse with me; but to this day, I don't know where I found the courage to recite this memory verse when *Aboi-abyin* cried against me in the river.

But *Aboi-abyin* did not go away. They cried even louder: 'Foolish child; we are your roots. You are our leaves. Can the leaves abandon its own roots and claim the roots of another tree and hope to prosper? Foolish child,' *Aboi-abyin* laughed in the most unearthly manner. I would die with that laughter still ringing in my head.

'I ... I ... I ... am sorry *Aboi-abyin*,' I whimpered. 'I ... I ... only told you wh-at my father taught me.'

'Your father is a foolish man and a coward,' cried *Aboi-abyin*. 'Go and tell him that we said he is a foolish man. A hunter he had never seen met him in his farm and gave him meat while pointing his arrow at him, and he carried his crops and farmland and gave the hunter. The piece of meat the hunter gave him took over his head and he could no longer think well. The hunter said to him, "leave farming and be a hunter like me," and he abandoned his hoe on the fertile land his fathers left for him to chase the wind with a nomadic hunter who does not know his own home and therefore respects nobody's home. The hunter is gone, but your father still looks upon farming with contempt though he was more prosperous in it. The terror of the hunter's arrow and the sweetness of his meat are still in his head with which he thinks stupid thoughts and in his mouth with which he speaks foolish things. What he thinks is light is a disease that has no cure. What he thinks is darkness is health that requires no cure. He is a fool and in the dark with all the light he thinks he has around him.'

'For-give me. I ... am sorry,' I sniffed

Aboi-abyin cried louder than before:

Owowowo Mbeeee woh
Woh Mbeeeee woh
Woh Mbeeeee woh
Woh Mbeeeee woh
Owowowo Mbeeee woh

Mbare was my great grandfather and like my grandfather, he was *Agwa-boi* in his own time. In fact, he was a greater and more revered *Agwa-boi* than my grandfather. People said he was the greatest *Agwa-boi* they had ever known. It was from him my grandfather inherited the revered office of *Agwa-boi*. The cry of *Aboi-abyin* in the river was a tearful lamentation of my father's betrayal of my great grandfather by converting to Christianity. For a while, my brain shut down. I was paralysed by fear. When I came to my senses, the first thing that came into my mind was that what my father taught me was indeed foolish and untrue as *Aboi-abyin* had said. If there was any truth in it, it was that *Aboi-abyin* was the unseen ears of the ground, the unseen eyes of the water and the unseen mouth of the trees. Here I was in this river seeing only water and trees, but hearing the cry of *Aboi-abyin* so close to me, yet I could not see them. How could I even say *Aboi-abyin* in whose water and on whose ground I was standing should walk away from his home? Christ and heaven where were they? I had seen *akrusak* and I had heard the eerie cry of *Aboi-byin*. Even now

27

where I stood I could see *akrusak* and hear the eerie cry of *Aboi-abyin*. Where was Christ and heaven? But I have heard *Aboi-abyin* the eyes of the water, if I have not seen them. Who knows if standing as I was in the water of river Yatuk, I had with my feet thrown sand into the eyes of the ancestors. I might even be standing on their eyes and their cry is a cry of pain. At this thought, I ran out of the river clutching at my chest in fear and pain.

As I ran, I could hear a fresh cry of *Aboi-abyin*:

Owowowo Mbeeee woh
Woh Mbeeeeee woh
Woh Mbeeeeee woh
Woh Mbeeeeee woh
Owowowo Mbeeee woh

When I had put a good distance between me and the river, I stopped running out of exhaustion and sat down under a tree beside the path, my face in the direction of the river. Now I could think better. Were the footsteps behind me the footsteps of *Aboi-abyin*? If they were, the ancestors would not have allowed me to reach the school. At the school, Zwahu had talked of me not being initiated into the Aboi-oracle. Had he sent the ancestors after me? But did he have the power to send the ancestors on such an errand? His father might still be in the Aboi-oracle and he himself might have been initiated into the oracle, I doubted his power to wake up the ancestors to terrorize me.

After I had rested, I continued my journey home. Now most of my fear was gone. With my fear gone, my thoughts returned once more to my headmaster and his powers. If I become a headmaster, I will build a big bridge over river Yatuk and construct a big road between Tyosa and Sarai. I will buy raincoats for my father and mother so they would not have to use the waterproof capes they wore in the rainy season.

As a child, I could only think of the powers of a headmaster without thinking of his limitations. My headmaster's motorcycle had just failed him and he could not repair it. He pushed it past me swearing and cursing in frustration. The other day he could not cross over a little stream with it because of a flood and had to walk to my village on foot. Yet, I could not think of any of these.

For two days after I returned from the primary school at Sarai, I was sick. I knew it was because of *Aboi-abyin*, but I could not tell my father. To tell him would mean telling him I disobeyed him. But I told my mother and begged her not to tell my father. I feared I was going to die and it seemed my mother had the same fear also. Between children and women, the fear of *Aboi-abyin* was a mortal one. Whenever *mapyia* – the bigheaded ancestor was passing in the night, I used to cling to my mother and she would cling to the wall of our room in fear.

By the evening of the second day, I began to regain my health, and by the third day, I was well again. On the third day, I went to my father and said I would like to be enrolled in primary school the next enrolment season.

'Have you forgotten the headmaster's rule against little fingers and little ears?' my father asked.

'No,' I said, feeling sad.

'Good,' said my father. 'Always remember the headmaster's rule against little fingers and little ears before you talk of enrolment into that school.'

Chapter Five

Little Fingers, Little Ears

Little fingers and little ears do not make the register of the school was an admission rule my headmaster insisted must not be breached in the admission of pupils into his primary school. In those days before you were admitted into Sarai primary school, the fingers of your right hand would have to touch your left ear. You would be asked to hold your head erect, not to tilt it to one side. Then your right hand would be passed over your head until your fingers or at least one of them touches your left ear. This showed you had reached school age. If none of your fingers could touch your left ear, you had not attained school age and must wait for the following year. Near my house, Daniel who was something of a dwarf with a big head was kept out of school for many years by this rule. Each year, his little hand was past over his big head, but in the words of Tagwai a jester in my village, Daniel's little hand would not even cross his big head to peep at his left ear on the other side of his head before it would come to an end only a little beyond the centre of his vast head. For many years, he was returned home to allow his hand to grow, but no one thought of shrinking his big head for his hand to touch his ear or at least peep at it. How my headmaster came by this admission requirement no one knew. It was a rule whose rationale my age could not understand nor account for. All I could think of then was that there must be a connection between the size of one's hands and ears with learning and understanding.

After my first visit to the primary school, I kept worrying my father that he must enrol me in school. I had always liked learning; but my visit to the school had sharpened that crave.

'But you are too young Nto,' my father kept saying. 'School is for grown ups.'

'I may be young, but you know I learn fast,' I would say.

'That I know,' my father would say. 'Still I think you are too young to go to school. 'You are only seven years old. Remember *little fingers and little ears don't make the school's register*.'

This was the repartee I dreaded most. It was a refrain of my older siblings already attending school and it was fast becoming a refrain of my father.

'Daddy, I really want to go to school, no matter,' I said to my father one day.

'Let's wait and hope your hands or your ears grow a little longer before the next school enrolment season,' my father said. As an afterthought, he said, 'come here Nto.'

I knew why I was being asked to come nearer to him. My heart was now beating slightly faster. When I moved close to where he was sitting, he extended his right hand and drew me closer to him. You did not draw a child to you with your left hand. You did not even receive food or any gift with your left hand and a child was more precious than food or any gift. He stood up to begin a ritual he had performed on me almost as many times as I had requested I be enrolled in school.

'Hold your head erect,' he ordered.

I held my head upright.

He took my right hand and passed it over my head, but even my central finger could not touch my left ear. I strained to push my hand so that it could touch my ear, but it was all in vain. My central finger only touched my ear when I tilted my head to one side.

'Ah, you know that won't do,' cried my father. 'Not with Bamai as headmaster in Sarai primary school. He is such a strict man on issues like this.'

At the mention of my headmaster, my worry of not being able to go to Sarai primary school was replaced by fear. I could imagine how he would roll out his big eyeballs to stare at me after he had subjected me to his test and I failed to meet up. A man who would be cursing and swearing at his motorcycle may do worse things to human beings who should know better than ask him for what they knew was not their due.

When my father looked at my face and saw how frightened and dejected I looked, he quickly added, 'but you don't need to worry too much. It is still a long way off to the next enrolment season. Who knows, before that time you would have grown more and your hand would be able to touch your ear.'

That night I didn't sleep well. If only there was another primary school nearby, I would have asked my father to take me there instead of facing my headmaster and his eyes and his implacable rule against *little ears* and *little fingers*. But there was no other primary school nearby. The only primary school that could be said to be nearby was that at Fakkan and that was some nine kilometres away from my village. I could not conceivably trek that distance twice every day, and worse – trek it alone since no child of Tyosa went to that school. How was I even sure a similar rule did not exist at Fakkan? How was I even sure there was no another Bamai there as headmaster applying the rule without pity and terrorising little children like me with his big eyeballs?

Chapter Six

The Hawk, the Chick and the Vulture

For about two weeks after my headmaster pushed his motorcycle past where I was hiding on the day of my adventure to Sarai primary school, he was not seen on his motorcycle but on a bicycle. That my headmaster was now riding a bicycle meant he had not repaired the motorcycle. The motorcycle must have developed serious mechanical problems that he may have to take it to Zonkwa for repairs. Some people said its engine had knocked. Most people before now did not know he had a bicycle because he had not been seen riding it.

Now my headmaster came to my village quietly without the usual motorcycle noise that usually heralded his coming. People knew he was around only when they saw him. I could imagine how even the birds of the forest would be happy now that they were not subjected to the noise of the motorcycle. But the pigs were now more in danger of an accident with my headmaster. However, it turned out I was the one to have an accident with my headmaster on his bicycle before the pigs.

A week after my adventure to the school, I was pushing the old rim of a balkanised bicycle on the small path behind our house when I bumped into my headmaster riding his bicycle on the same path on his way to the forest after our village to inspect his guinea fowl traps.

Pushing a bicycle rim with a stick always entailed running. In fact, the rim was pushed by children to make them run. Often when a child was sent on errand, if he had such a rim, it would help him run the errand faster. On this day that I bumped into my headmaster, I had just run an errand for my mother to Sank'aniet and was returning home. Well, it was not exactly my mother's errand. It was in fact my errand. Sank'aniet was a woman that would never pay her debts. She owed my mother five kobo, but would not pay. My mother was the sort of person that would not pester her over the money. So she told me if I could collect the debt from Sank'aniet, I could spend the money. My mother knew how importunate I could be and that was why she assigned the debt to me. Each day I would go to Sank'aniet's house three times asking for my mother's money. When I bumped into my headmaster's bicycle I was returning from Sank'aniet's house where I had finally collected the money from her.

As soon as she had seen me entering the house, she had cried out: 'Ah, this boy. If you are sent to *eat* anybody by witchcraft, the person will not last a day. Take your mother's money and never set your feet in this house again,' she said, flinging the money at me. I picked the money on the ground where she flung it and headed back home happy I had succeeded where my mother had failed. I was in such a jubilant mood that I was reckless in the way I was propelling my bicycle rim forward.

The path was a small meandering path that unless my eyes were on the rim I was pushing, I could easily go off the path. My eyes were fixed on the rim I was pushing, my head in the air full of happiness and plans of how I would spend the money I had just collected from Sank'aniet. As soon as I rounded up a bend, my rim collided with my headmaster's bicycle and I avoided collision with the bicycle by a reflex that made me jump into the bush.

'*Waih, waih, kai, wuu!*' cried my headmaster as he brought his feet down from the bicycle's pedals in an attempt to avoid falling off the bicycle. But it was in vain. The bicycle went off the path and threw my headmaster off on a *sunsom* shrub where my rim was lying. He fell on the rim and cried out, '*waih!*'

Not knowing what to do, I stood watching him trying to roll clear of the shrub. After he rolled clear of the shrub, I could see him holding the left side of his abdomen by the ribs. I suspected that was the part of his body that landed more heavily on my bicycle rim.

'This boy!' this boy! What a naughty boy! What a rascally boy,' he groaned. I stood looking at him too terrified to even run away. He also stood looking at me without making to get hold of me for causing an accident I might have prevented if I were more careful and less reckless with excitement. But when his eyes fell on my clenched fist where I was holding the five kobo I collected from Sank'aniet, I could see them narrowing to a scowl.

My mother had taught me never to put money in my pocket as the pocket might have a hole through which the money could easily get lost. Instead of putting it in a pocket, I should hold it in my hand and I could be sure of not losing it. So I was holding the money I had collected from Sank'aniet in my hand. My headmaster by the look on his face must be wondering what I was clenching so tightly in my left hand that had turned it into a fist that a man with a bad mind would have thought was a fist I meant to fight him with.

'What are you holding in that hand?' he asked, glowering at me.

'It is money my mother sent me to collect from her debtor,' I said, my voice trembling.

Suspicion crept into his face that would never lose its terror on me.

'Are you a debt collector?' he asked.

I did not say anything. My silence only served to deepen his suspicion.

'Tell me the truth. Did you steal the money?'

I was alarmed by this question and started trembling. This hardened his suspicion into belief. It was then he lumbered towards me. In his mind I believed he thought he was coming to arrest a little thief that must not be allowed to grow into a big thief. As he lumbered towards me, I had the horrifying feeling I was a chick and he was a hawk coming to devour me. I looked round for my mother or father as a chick would look for the wings of its mother when the hawk swoops down on it. But neither my father nor mother were there to protect me. My headmaster seized my little hand and drawing me very close to him, bared his eyeballs at me. I shut my eyes and began to cry. I tried to wrest my hand out of his grip, but his hold was firm. He held me with one hand, dragged me to where his bicycle was lying and raised it with one hand. He asked me where our house was and I pointed at our house. Holding the bicycle with one hand and my little hand with the other, he started walking towards our house.

As we walked to my house, my headmaster's eyes kept straying to my clenched hand which was the hand he was holding. But never for once did he attempt opening my hand to confirm it was money I was holding and how much was the money. He seemed satisfied I was holding money and it was stolen money. It did not matter how much the money was. My parents must know of the little thief they have and they must watch him as he punishes me before their eyes to purge the bad seed in me that must not be allowed to germinate and grow into a sturdy tree. My headmaster was the discipline master of the village. He did not report erring children to their parents. It was the parents that reported their erring children to my headmaster for discipline, particularly if they were already of school age and were attending his school. But even if they were not of school age, they could still be disciplined by my headmaster because eventually they would end up in his school and their discipline determined whether they were to be admitted or kept out of the school. My headmaster had the right to refuse admission to a child he felt was a bad child so that he did not come into the school to be a bad influence to other children. In the days of my headmaster, a child was not only the child of his parents, but everyone's child. Thus if a man met children playing in their farm instead of working because their father was not in the farm with them, he could beat them up and their father on hearing what the man had done would go to thank him.

To return to my accident with my headmaster, my heart kept plunging down in fear as my headmaster led me home, though I knew I was innocent of what he suspected.

'Your mother sent you to collect her debt for her, since when did you become a debt collector?' I heard my headmaster asking me as he walked me home.

'True sir, the money is her money that Sank'aniet owed her,' I whined.

'True,' murmured my headmaster. 'Little child, you should know that debt collectors and tax collectors are not to be trusted to have the truth with them. Remember Zachaeus the tax collector was a sinner until he repented of his sins of tax collection. You can even remember what the publican said about the tax collector that was praying with him in the synagogue. Though Christ condemned the self-righteous attitude of the publican, but we can see that what he was saying of the tax collector was true. The tax collector was so weighed down by his sins that he was not even able to lift up his head to look at the altar before which he knelt to pray. Indeed even Jesus did not say the tax collector was anything near clean. All he said was that the sanctimonious attitudes of the publican were not good for his spiritual growth. You may say you are not a tax collector but a debt collector. But you can only say so because you are a child. A tax collector himself is a debt collector, collecting what the people owe to the government. And do you know something little boy? I don't even believe you have collected any debt for your mother. Why should she send a little boy like you to collect her debt for her?'

'True sir, the money with me is her money that Sank'aniet owed her,' I whined.

'At least that is your story,' said my headmaster. ''It will remain your story until your mother says so. Who can trust little children of nowadays? If you can bump into elders without respect, how are you to be trusted to pass money by?'

'True it is my mother's money.'

'Until your mother says so.'

My parents were surprised to see me and my headmaster walked into our house with my headmaster holding my hand. To my knowledge, it was the first time he entered our house. Before now, all he had done was to ride his motorcycle past our house, never stopping to talk to anyone; never even acknowledging the waving hands of people on his way of passage. But today he was in our house and in a very disagreeable manner.

Both my father and mother were at home when my headmaster and I came into the house. It was a Saturday a non-school day. All my older siblings were at home also. As soon as they saw my headmaster, all of them started saying, 'Good morning sir,' and bowing down at the same time. He waved his hand at them without saying anything. The moment they finished greeting him, they all disappeared from the house. Out of respect and reverence for teachers, no child remained in his house if any of his teachers paid a visit to his house. When my father greeted my headmaster, he greeted him back, though in a brittle voice.

'What is the matter headmaster?' my father asked my headmaster, his voice full of alarm.

'Are you his father?' my headmaster asked in a voice that only served to throw my father into more alarm.

The moment my mother who was in her room knitting her mat while waiting for the food she was cooking heard this question of my headmaster, she came out of her room. My mother was a very busy woman. She had no moment of rest from the time she woke up in the morning to the time she went back to sleep at night. I always marvelled at her strength. When she came out of her room, she greeted my headmaster and he answered her in a voice that sounded hostile to me. She stood looking at us wondering what was the matter.

'Yes, I am his father,' my father answered my headmaster. 'What has he done?' he asked in a voice that carried his feelings.

'Your son has stolen somebody's money. I brought him before you to find out whose money it is and how much is the money?' my headmaster declared in the most matter-of-fact fashion. 'Now someone should go and bring me a cane.'

My mind jumped to Sankwai. Certainly he must be lurking somewhere craving for this kind of errand. He would find a sturdy stick that would eat into my flesh to get back at me for depriving him of his meat. But to my surprise, Sankwai did not appear with a stick nor did any of my other siblings. Perhaps Sankwai was not hiding behind the house as I had suspected; in fact almost believed. Perhaps he has actually fled the house as my other siblings apparently did. Later, however, it occurred to me that even if Sankwai or other siblings of mine were lurking somewhere near the house, they won't dare run this errand of my headmaster because doing so would give them away as pupils that were not adhering to the courtesy of leaving their house when their teacher – their headmaster for that matter, was in their house. How were they to know that my headmaster's request was not a ploy to make them give themselves away as rebels of convention?

My headmaster looking round and not seeing anyone to carry out his instruction began to unbuckle his belt which he would use to whip me.

My father looked at me horrified. 'Nto is it true what the headmaster had said?' he asked.

'No it is not true,' I said, hastily. 'The money is my mother's money with Sank'niet,' I cried, cowering away from my headmaster who still held my hand. I was looking up pleadingly at my mother to confirm my story.

My mother for sometime could not say anything. Sank'aniet was such a difficult debtor she found it difficult to believe I had succeeded in collecting the debt from her. But she knew I was not a thief. 'How much is the money with you?' she asked me finally.

'Five kobo,' I said unclenching my fist to show them the money in my hand.

'What Nto is saying is true,' my mother said to my headmaster. Though she believed me, there was still something of a plea in her voice.

Woman don't turn the child into a debt collector,' my headmaster admonished my mother in a very stern voice while releasing his hold on me. 'You go to church more than I do and therefore should know it is not good for his soul,' my headmaster continued his sermon. 'Don't expose him to money. It would contaminate him. Remember money is the root of all evil. You know how Jesus drove out the money changers out of the temple. You should know more than me.'

Without further word to my mother or father, my headmaster took his bicycle, which he had reclined against the wall of my father's room, and rode out of our house, leaving me more mystified by who he was.

For a long time, I remained standing where my headmaster left me feeling my wrist where he had held me for any bruises he might have caused. At the same time, I was thinking of Zwahu. For that day, meat was to be cooked in our house and I might have to part with it to him if I must continue to count on him to keep my secret. The hawk has departed and in its place a vulture now perched looking greedily at me while its throat raced up and down in gluttonous anticipation.

Chapter Seven

The Missing Number

The next school enrolment season my father took me to the school to be enrolled. Before taking me however, he once more performed the ritual of passing his right hand over my head to see if it would touch my left ear. Knowing the ritual would be performed on the day I would be taken to school, I had been performing it alone in preparation. The first day I performed it, none of my fingers touched my ear. The second day it was the same thing. Panic started gripping me. Does it mean I would not be enrolled in school this year again? No, I must be enrolled this year I told myself. I would do anything to ensure that. I got grip of myself and began flexing my hands, particularly my right hand, and pulling my fingers particularly the fingers of my right hand. I would pull each finger until it gave a snapping sound before going to the next. I did this for two days. On the third day, I was surprised to find the central finger of my right hand was touching my left ear. I was elated. I would be in school this year. Having achieved this, when my father asked me to come over on the day he was taking me to school for him to perform the ritual, I went to him without fear.

But to my dismay when my father performed the ritual on me, none of my fingers could touch my ear. I was alarmed and perplexed. What was happening to me? Was it because in my wild anticipation of enrolment in the school I did not perform the ritual the previous day that my central finger can no longer touch my ear or could the problem be with the way my father was performing the ritual? That must be the problem. So I told my father to allow me do it myself.

My father shrugged his shoulders and stepped away from me to see what magic I would perform.

I flexed my hands and pulled my fingers as I used to do and under the watchful eyes of my father passed my right hand over my head and behold my central finger was touching my left ear.

My father was surprised. Thinking I must have slightly tilted my head to one side to achieve the astonishing result, he asked me to repeat the ritual so he could watch me more closely.

I did and he could see I had not played any trick. He seemed much happy with the result I had achieved than myself. 'Congratulations my son,' he said, cuddling me to him. 'You are now a pupil of Sarai primary school.'

I thanked him and we set out for Sarai with faith and confidence that I had nothing to worry over again concerning my admission.

But neither I nor my father bargained with the fact that my headmaster would not only insist on measuring my hand against my ear by himself, but would ask me to count the English numerals from 1 to 10. It was only in the school we found this out.

That morning, we were about seven children brought by our parents to be enrolled in the school. In the order we arrived the school, we queued in front of my headmaster's office. Our parents that brought us were seated far away from us. My headmaster was inside the office carrying out the admission test into his school. On the queue outside, I was the last of the seven because I arrived last. We were called into the office one after the other by my headmaster himself. When a child entered the office, he would close the door behind the child and it was only open when he was through with the child. None of us had an idea of what was going on inside the office. It was to me like an initiation into the Aboi-oracle. A child was carried shrieking and kicking into the little shrine to be initiated into the Aboi-oracle. No one outside the shrine knew what was happening to the child inside the shrine and the child when he came out did not tell anyone his ordeal inside the shrine.

The first three children on the queue had no problem. They all came out of my headmaster's office smiling in satisfaction that they were now pupils of Sarai primary school. But they did not speak to any of us yet to enter the office. They walked away without even bidding us farewell.

Unlike the first three children however, the fourth child came out of my headmaster's office crying. It was clear he had failed the test being administered inside the office. Like the other children before him, he walked away without bidding us farewell; though in his case, it was understandable having not fared well himself.

All of us were now apprehensive. The looks of confidence hitherto on our faces started withering and were replaced with looks of fear and uncertainty. As was the case with the fourth child, the fifth child also came out of my headmaster's office in tears. The two of us still on the line exchanged glances of fear. A passing wind sang an eerie song that sounded like the song of *Aboi-abyin* in my ears and I jumped up in fear. The sixth child entered the office leaving me alone outside. He came out smiling. But his smile did not comfort me much. Haven't I seen two children came out of my headmaster's office crying? Who said I might not make the third child?

My headmaster beckoned me in and I braced myself for the worst. My headmaster's office was a very small office with hardly a space to swing a cat. The only window in the office was a small one and it did not even appear to be in the direction of the wind's flow. Perhaps it was because of lack of space in the office that we had to queue outside. My headmaster no doubt looked bigger than his office. It would not be surprising to me that much of his sweating was caused by this small, airless office. When he was in it, he sweated. When he was out of it, he sweated, perhaps imagining he was in it. Except for the fact that it was square in shape, there were many ways in which the office reminded me of the *Aboi* shrine in Tyosa.

Under the small window of the small office was my headmaster's table and chair. On the left side of the table was a bench with uneven stands. When you sit on the bench, it would pitch you forward before regaining its balance, with your help no doubt. While sitting on the bench, you have to be doing a delicate balancing act with your feet on the floor and your buttocks on the bench. I sat on the bench and was pitched forward, but my feet on the floor stabilized the bench. My headmaster was scribbling something on his table which appeared not to enjoy a better balance than the bench I was sitting on. Whenever he shifted his weight on the chair he was sitting, the chair emitted a string of quaking noise. My headmaster's hand was flying over the paper he was writing and I marvelled at his writing expertise. The beauty of his writing stood in sharp contrast with the sullied state of his office. I could not imagine that one day I would be able to write like that.

When my headmaster had finished writing, he stood up and regarded me coldly. Involuntarily I looked down to avoid his eyes.

'What is your name?' he asked, his eyes boring holes into my face.

'Nto,' I replied.

'Your father's name.'

'Kwasau.'

He wrote something on a piece of paper before him and I took it that it was my name he wrote.

'Why do you want to be admitted into Sarai primary school?' he asked me, quite unexpectedly.

'So that I can write like you,' I answered.

From the light that flowed into his face, I could see he was happy with my reply. 'You seemed to be a clever boy,' he said.

I did not say anything.

'Stand up and let me see how far your hand goes to your ear,' he said at the same time giving me a-stand-up gesture.

I stood up and quickly passed my right hand over my head and my central finger touched my left ear. I trust my ability to perform this ritual on myself than anyone performing it on me.

'That won't do,' my headmaster said. 'I do the measurement not you.' Saying this, he quickly detached himself from the little table he had stood by as if it had suddenly turned into a snake that was rearing its head at him and moved towards me. He took my right hand with his left hand and passed it over my head while holding my head erect with his right hand.

I stretched my central finger to a painful point and to my happiness my central finger still touched my left ear.

'This would do,' said my headmaster, nodding his head at the same time to convey by action what he had already said to me with his lips.

I made to go out of the office.

'One more thing,' my headmaster said, fixing his eyes on my face. Our eyes met and panic began to seize my mind. His eyeballs looking bigger now were eating up my face.

'Recite the English numerals from 1 to 10,' he said.

Still in my panic, I started reciting the numerals, but whenever I got to number 9, I could not recall the number. Unable to remember it, I would jump to 10.

'One number is missing,' my headmaster said.

'Yes, I know,' I said, raking my brains to recall the missing number, but could not on the spur of the moment.

'That number is critical,' said my headmaster, looking critical himself.

'Yes sir,' I said, fear gnawing at my heart.

'It can deny you admission.'

I was now thoroughly scared and without further prompting by my headmaster I started reciting the numerals again. But when I got to 9 again I could not remember the number.

'You can go,' said my headmaster, dismissing me with his hand. 'By next year I believe you would be able to recall the number you cannot recall now. Then your father can bring you again for enrolment.'

I did not move. I remained where I was and started crying.

My headmaster again fixed his eyes on me. I don't know from where I got the courage, but I met his gaze this time. As his eyes remained on me, the expression on his face began to change from its severe complexion to something mild, even friendly. 'You look like the boy I collided with his bicycle rim in Tyosa about a year ago,' he said finally

'I am he,' I said still crying.

'The boy I thought was lying to me about the money in his hand.'

I nodded my head.

'The boy I thought was a thief, but found he was not.'

'I nodded my head again.

'You are an honest child.'

I did not say anything.

'For your honesty and the courage I find in you, you will be admitted into the school this year,' he said, smiling at me. 'When you come here, you would learn to recite the numerals,' he said, waving me away and returning to sit down on his chair behind the table.

I ran out of the office gliding like a swooping kite. Tears and swirls of wind twirled round my ears, but now their songs were *zunzom* music to me.

Chapter Eight

To Every Teacher His Due

On my first day in school, my headmaster gathered all the new intakes and introduced our teachers to us. There were six classes in the school and there were nine teachers. My headmaster was the tenth teacher.

From class one to three, the teachers were fixed. They did not rotate. Each teacher was assigned to teach a class. In those classes, a teacher taught all the subjects of his class. So he was supposed to know all the subjects of the class which were mainly English, arithmetic, social studies and drawing. Ordinarily my headmaster was not supposed to teach but to take care of the administration of the school. But he combined his administrative duties with teaching. He would go to any class to teach any subject at any time. He knew all subjects and was a very good teacher. Though he entered every class to teach, he more often went to class one and three. Class one because he said new intakes deserved special handling and he was the one to give the special handling. Class three because Malachy the teacher in that class was not a good teacher. He did not know the class subjects very well and had a bad methodology of teaching any subject. Even his handwriting was not good. His pupils said it was like marks left behind in the dust by a writhing earthworm. Though my headmaster knew these, he had never been heard or seen talking to Malachy to improve his knowledge and his teaching methodology. If he talked to him, it must be in private.

Because Malachy could not teach well, his pupils did not often understand what he was teaching. But perhaps, some of his pupils did not understand his teaching because instead of listening, they made noise while he was teaching. Their noise scarcely bothered Malachy. He was a teacher who hardly got angry at anyone.

One day Malachy was teaching in his class and one of the pupils went under his desk and started crying like a cat. Malachy went on with his teaching as if nothing was happening. Another day he was teaching and another pupil started drumming loudly on his desk, Malachy ignored him. Yet another day he was teaching and a pupil started whistling loudly distracting other pupils, Malachy continued teaching unperturbed. But this pupil was not as lucky as the others. My headmaster was then passing by the class. Usually he used to move round the classes to see the teachers teaching and the pupils learning. Passing by a class, he would peep in either through the door or an open window to inspect what was going on in the class. It was when he was walking past Malachy's class that this pupil had the misfortune of whistling. My headmaster heard and saw him whistling.

'Who are those whistling in class?' he asked, coming into the class.

Malachy stopped teaching and a hush fell over the class. Whichever class my headmaster entered, a deafening silence always descended on it. Then it was only his voice to be heard.

'I said who is the hunter I heard whistling and who is his dog?' my headmaster asked again. Without waiting for an answer, he went to the pupil who was whistling and pulled him up by the ear. 'Why were you whistling?'

Everyone was shocked. How did my headmaster know the pupil who was whistling? He was not in the class when the pupil was whistling. This was the sort of thing that made pupils say my headmaster was a wizard. One day he was walking with his back to the classes towards a church building not far from the school and a pupil in class had the audacity of calling his name so loudly that he heard him. He did not turn, but walked on to the church. When he returned, he walked to the pupil inside his classroom and asked why he was calling him. The pupil nearly fainted out of fear. How did my headmaster know he was the one who called his name? The pupil that whistled in Malachy's class was now in the same position. Like the other pupil, he was trembling with fear.

'Are you deaf?' my headmaster shouted at him, baring his eyeballs.

The pupil cowered away from him and began to cry.

My headmaster pulled him out to the front of the class. Whenever he wanted to discipline any pupil, he did it either in front of the school assembly or in front of the pupil's class so that other pupils who saw the erring pupil being punished would be deterred from treading his path. Whether a student would be punished in front of his class or the school assembly often depended on how my headmaster viewed his offence. If he viewed it as a serious offence, the pupil would be punished in front of the assembly. But if he considered it a mild offence, it would be in front of the pupil's class.

When he took the whistling pupil to the front of the class, he asked him to lie down on the teacher's table.

The pupil lay down on his stomach.

'Class monitor get me a cane outside.' It was a deliberate command. Other pupils would be loathed to bring a cane that would be used to flog their classmate as doing so would make the pupil being punished to hate them. But the class monitor was in charge of the discipline of the class and he could do so without fearing challenge from anybody. Beside, he was a big boy no one dared challenge.

The class monitor ran out and soon was back to class with a slim though sturdy branch of a eucalyptus tree.

'Now I am going to give you seven lashes of the cane on your buttocks so that next time when you want to whistle, your buttocks would advise your mouth against it. The pupil's trousers were pulled down so that the cane would land on his bare buttocks with maximum effect. Each time the cane landed, the pupil cried out in pain and his hands would flail about his buttocks trying to relieve the pain. On each landing of the cane, my headmaster called out the number of the lash until he had completed the seven lashes. When he was through, the pupil came down from the teacher's table crying and made for his seat. But my headmaster held him back.

'My friend, this is not a hunting society,' said my headmaster. 'If you want to whistle, visit the hunters in the bush. Idiot! Now go.'

The pupil went back to his seat sniffing. My headmaster walked out of the classroom and Malachy resumed his teaching in a quieter class.

When my headmaster gathered us the new entrants in the school to introduce the school teachers to us, after introducing each teacher by his name, the class and subjects he was teaching, he told us we should know that the teachers were now our new parents. Any disrespect to them was disrespect to our parents at home and it would be dealt with by him. Part of our responsibility to the teachers was to keep their compound clean and in a habitable condition.

All the teachers lived in the same compound. It was a-face-me-I-face-you premises. All the apartments were double rooms and thatched. But my headmaster lived in a separate house from the teachers. While the teachers had only two rooms, my headmaster had about four rooms in his house. But like the teachers, my headmaster's house was also thatched. The school pupils cut the grass for thatching the teachers' compound and my headmaster's house. They also went to the river to fetch the bamboo sticks, the raffia and other forest growths needed to thatch my headmaster's house and the teachers' compound. My headmaster insisted that the thatch on his house and the teachers' compound must be replaced after every two years to avoid leaking during the rainy season. Whenever pupils were going to the river to fetch bamboo and raffia, my headmaster insisted that a teacher accompanied them to the river to ensure no pupil was wounded or suffered any harm in the river. The older pupils did the thatching. If a new building was to be erected, the younger pupils fetched the water for the making of the mud while the bigger pupils make the mud and lay the bricks.

A year before my admission into Sarai primary school, the roof of Malachy's room was blown off by the wind and rain fell in the room and on his house effects about the same way it fell outside. The room was thatched in the dry season preceding that rainy season. My headmaster said the roof was blown off because it was not properly thatched. The older boys who did the thatching did not bind well the pillars that held the thatch to the mud ceiling and did not also bind well the thatch to the bamboo sticks that intermingled with the pillars. That was why a wind that was not strong blew the roof apart. He called an assembly to address the matter. The older pupils who did the thatching of the room were brought to the front of the assembly for chastisement. My headmaster was standing on the veranda in front of his office with all the teachers behind him while their pupils were lined up in front of them according to their classes.

'What has happened to Malachy's room is very bad,' my headmaster said. 'People would want to see it as an act of God, but I am seeing it as the wicked act of man. We should leave God out of it and see what happened for what it truly is – the negligence and carelessness of some irresponsible people in our midst. If we bring God into it, we will be committing a second sin of blaming God for what he did not do after our first sin of not doing what we should have done. The pupils standing in front of us today were the pupils who thatched Malachy's roof the previous dry season. I brought them to the front of the assembly to explain to us how a roof they thatched less than five months ago should be blown off by a rainstorm that could not raise the hair on my head in any sensible form when older roofs did not even know there was a rainstorm. Michael, why did you not thatch Malachy's room well?' he asked the tallest among the pupils who thatched the room.

Many people had doubted whether the roof was blown off because it was not properly thatched. But to their shock, the pupils who were being blamed by my headmaster for the disaster started trading accusations at each other when my headmaster demanded to know why they failed to thatch the roof properly. Michael said he told one of his fellows to put enough mud on the base of the pillar, but the fellow refused. The fellow Michael was accusing said it was all Michael's fault because he did not knot the pillars well and when he was asked to re-knot them, he refused. My headmaster no doubt was a wizard to have so easily gotten to the truth of the cause of the disaster.

'Now that you have confessed to your crime,' said my headmaster, 'will you say you have given Mr. Malachy his due as your teacher?'

Michael and the other pupils shook their heads.

'Will you even say you have given him his due as a human being?'

Again the accused pupils shook their heads.

'Did you want to kill him?'

Nobody said anything.

'Do you know that in Babylon anyone that committed a crime like this would be hanged by his neck until he died and even God would not have mercy on his soul?'

Most of the pupils wondered where Babylon was because until that day, few of them had ever heard the name of a place bearing that name.

'Why did you do what you did?' my headmaster asked in a tone more severe than before. Is it because Mr. Malachy is such a simple, forgiving person?'

No one said anything.

'Let me tell you something my friends. Even if Mr. Malachy would forgive or overlook this, I will not. I owe responsibility to this school that my pupils discharge their duties to those such duties are due. I have told you how a criminal who committed this kind of crime was punished in Babylon. What punishment would you have me inflict on such offenders in our school?' my headmaster asked the assembly.

Nobody spoke. All the pupils and teachers knew he already had in mind what punishment to mete out on the offenders and so it was pointless for a teacher prescribing any and for the pupils, it was unthinkable.

'If you don't know I will tell you,' said my headmaster, peremptorily. 'For a whole week, such offenders would work in the school farm after classes. That is my punishment for you. In addition, your parents would have to find a house for Mr. Malachy and pay for any property he lost to the rain. Mr Malachy, do you have anything to say?'

Mr Malachy stepped forward from behind my headmaster. Since the pupils knew him, they had never seen him wore such a mournful look. 'These pupils are like my younger brothers,' he said in a sad voice. 'I hate causing pain to them, but I don't know why they like causing pain to me. 'I ...' he trailed off and stepped back again behind my headmaster.

Some pupils were so moved by Mr. Malachy's pitiful countenance and what he said that they wept.

'You can go to your classes,' my headmaster said, waving the pupils in the assembly away. 'But those on whom I had passed my judgment should stay behind.'

After close of school that day, other pupils going home saw those my headmaster had found culpable for the blowing off of Malachy's roof carrying hoes and heading to the school farm. Their sentence had already commenced.

Chapter Nine

Eyes in the House

Since I was enrolled in the primary school, the eyes of my headmaster followed me everywhere I went at school or at home. His eyes were like *ajujoi* to me. *Ajujoi* was the spine-tingling song with which the ancestors were brought from the land of the dead to the *Aboi* shrine at the centre of the village during the *Aboi* festival. The living who would bring the ancestors to the small shrine left the village towards dusk the previous day for the forest where they stayed throughout the night. Towards dawn the following day, they arrived the village with the ancestors singing *ajujoi*:

Atyo ashi mavak ani gu tabyang
Ka alak, tak gu na lat akabagh:

Let he who is on the road step aside
Else his leg would not amount to much
In the calabash it would be eaten.

Ajujoi started as the song with which the ancestors were brought to the *Aboi* shrine for the *Aboi* festival, but ended up as a war cry and an oracle of discipline among the Atyap people. It was not a play song little children sang in the village playground at night, but a war song sung by men who had seen life and death. When men were going to war, they sang *ajujoi* and it gave courage to their hearts and strength to their arms. Those too weak to fight because of old age or sickness sang *ajujoi* crying out of anger and frustration for not being able to fight.

My headmaster often lamented that children and women were now wayward and irresponsible because *ajujoi* now was not as reproving of bad behaviour as it was when he was a child. He used to tell us he was initiated into the Aboi-oracle, but never told us what happened to him inside the shrine. Instead, he spoke in a cryptic manner that shrouded his initiation in a secret and mystery non-initiates should never unravel. But when I grew up, I asked my father who was a Christian, but who had been initiated into the Aboi-oracle by his father what happened to a child in the *Aboi* shrine during initiation. My father told me that a child being initiated into the Aboi-oracle was held over a lake of fire inside the *Aboi* shrine while *ajujoi* was sung telling the spirit of stubbornness and delinquency in the child to come out and be consumed by the fire. Though my father was a Christian, I could see fear on his face and sense reluctance in his voice as he revealed this secret to me. I believe that when my headmaster was initiated into the Aboi-oracle and *ajujoi* was sung, the *ajujoi* entered his eyes which forbade every delinquent act in his pupils.

Before I was enrolled into the school, there was a night my mother returned home drunk with *burukutu* – a fermented liquor brewed from millet and guinea corn. She was given her food to eat. I had eaten mine, but was still hungry. There was no light in my mother's room and it was in her pitched dark room that she started eating her food. I sat on the floor and was eating the food with her without her knowing. Soon the food was finished. My mother was surprised the food had finished so soon. She grumbled few words of an incoherent complaint and soon was asleep. I listened to her in the dark, smiling mischievously to myself.

After I was enrolled in the primary school, pranks like this ceased. The eyes of my headmaster were always hanging out there in the dark forbidding mischief in me. House chores which in my delinquency I used to dodge before I was enrolled in school, I now attended to religiously – because wherever I turned at home, I saw the eyes of my headmaster that were like *ajujoi* to me.

Towards the end of the rainy season, we used to go to our millet farm far away from the village to keep at bay monkeys that used to invade the farm. We paired ourselves for this task and kept watch over the farm on alternate days. On school days, we went to the farm after school. On non-school days, we went to the farm early in the morning when the grasses were still laden with dew.

Seven weeks after my enrolment into the primary school, Taciyah my elder brother and I were playing on our way to our millet farm to keep the monkeys off suddenly I saw the eyes of my headmaster dangling before me. Impulsively I started singing:

Dhere dhere dhere Agwai ooo owo wo (in English?)
Awaat nyiang na anat ajiniwo   (In English?)
ooo owo wo
Nwaat nyiang na nnaat chok zuk ooo owo wo
A chok zuk ji uhwa hwa ya ji
Ooo owo wo
Nchok zuk ji zyam jay a ji
Ooo owo wo
Ooo owo wo agwai o
Ooo owo wo
Baman jangata agwai ooo owo wo
Yali nat tankon agwai ooo owo wo
Nattankon nyhuoo owo wo
Owo wo agwai ooo owo wo
Dhere!

This was a song we used to sing to keep us company on our way to the farm and to keep our minds on the task before us. It was the pathetic song of a little child having to leave home and walk through the heavy early morning dew to go to farm to watch over the millet in the farm so that it was not devoured by monkeys which were always ravaging fields of millet in the bush.

When I started singing the song, Taciyah joined me and I thought the eyes of my headmaster must have appeared to him also. The eyes of my headmaster left me and perhaps Taciyah, but later returned to see if we were attending to our duty of watching over the millet. Towards evening, we left the farm and returned home. There was a farm of maize around the house. I saw some birds picking the seeds off the cobs. The eyes of my headmaster appeared again and I began to sing to scare the birds away:

> *O Kaman owo......... (In English)*
> *O lili bai aji...............(In English?)*
> *Gwanzwang Gwanzwang Makeri*
> *Nan nang akum dung aji*
> *Tso swaat na fui ma dong*
> *Nshoi baman tabo nu*
> *Owo wo hah!*

After I had scared away the birds, it was time to chase little goats that were yet to be on the leash into their hut for the night. Again the eyes of my headmaster appeared before me and I began to sing:

> *Kyat kyat kyat oo ......(In English?)*
> *Bagonzon kyat oo*
> *Yalinat oo*
> *Bagon zon kyat oo*
> *Kyat kyat kyat oo*
> *Bagon zon kyat oo*

As I sang this song, it reminded me of the timekeeper and his bell. As the timekeeper rang the school bell to tell pupils to assemble or go home, my song was telling the little goats to enter their pen in the far recess of the house for the night. I believed as I was frightened by the eyes of my headmaster at home to perform my duties, the timekeeper was frightened by the eyes of my headmaster to dutifully attend to his bell.

Chapter Ten

The Timekeeper and His Bell

The timekeeper of Sarai Primary School when I was admitted into the school was a frail looking boy whose house was very close to the school. Usually, school prefects were appointed among primary six pupils with their assistants appointed among primary five pupils. It was the policy of the school to appoint as timekeeper only pupils who lived close to the school. Perhaps looking for a sturdy pupil in class six living close to the school and not finding any, my headmaster appointed this fragile looking boy to whom the school bell appeared, in my eyes, to be a dead weight. The reason for the inflexible policy that the timekeeper must live close to the school was clear. Near the school, there was a railway iron bar hanging from an *alavam* tree. Each school day, the timekeeper went to strike the iron bar telling school pupils far and near to come to school. Like the talking-drum, the school iron bar was a talking-iron bar. When struck by the timekeeper, it said to the school pupils:

> Children, come to school
> Children, come to school.

The timekeeper performed the ritual of hitting the iron bar twice before ringing the big school bell which was a call to pupils to assembly. He struck the iron bar so early in the morning that he conceivably could not live far from it and be expected to discharge this responsibility. But living close to the iron bar, he came to strike it to inform others to prepare for school and he would go back home to prepare for school himself. He came back once more to give a final warning and went back home to eat his breakfast and pick his books and come to school. The bell he rang was not to tell anyone to come to school, but to tell those who had heeded the call of his iron bar and came to school to assemble. That was why instead of the bell saying, *children, come to school, children, come to school*, as the iron bar did; the bell simply screamed, 'assemble!' The bell was also a talking-bell.

There was only one clock in the school and it was by the timekeeper's side. Only my headmaster and a few teachers had wrist watches. Apart from ringing the bell to tell pupils to assemble, the timekeeper also rang the bell to mark the end of an hour and to tell teachers to switch onto other subjects from the ones they were teaching in the hour that had just run out. When rang to tell teachers an hour had ended, the bell gave three, distinct notes. When rang to tell pupils it was break-time or that school was over, it was a long, riotous shrill.

Whenever the timekeeper was ringing his bell or striking the iron bar with the iron rod, I always had the feeling that these tools of his office were too heavy for him. Yet he seemed to carry these tools with relative ease. Holding the bell with both hands, he would be snapping it up and down. A snap up seemed to lift him up from the ground and a snap down seemed to bring him back to the ground. In class, the bell was by the window where he sat. Whenever there was no teacher in their class, he would be pulling the tongue of the bell and rolling it between his fingers. One day a pupil carried the bell from the window where the timekeeper kept it and began to ring it in a long, riotous shrill that told pupils that it was break-time. Pupils thinking it was break-time, poured out of their classes. The moment the boy who rang the bell saw this, he put the bell back on the window and ran away before the timekeeper could get hold of him.

My headmaster on hearing the bell came charging into the class to know why the timekeeper should ring the bell when it was not break-time.

'Sir, it was not me who rang the bell,' said the timekeeper, fear besieging his face.

'Who rang it?' my headmaster asked

'I don't know his name sir,' said the timekeeper. 'But it is one tall boy. He has run away.'

'We will fish him out,' said my headmaster. 'But you will also be punished. It is your responsibility to take care of the bell and not allow anybody to reach it. The world is a place of responsibility,' he continued with a profound expression on his face. 'If you neglect your responsibility and something goes wrong, you have to take whatever comes to you. It is the responsibility of the school to provide a bell which we have provided. As timekeeper it is your responsibility to use the bell and take care of it which you seem to be failing at. You will have to dance to the music your irresponsibility is playing.'

Before school closed that day, my headmaster called an assembly to punish the timekeeper and the boy who rang the bell. At the assembly, the boy who rang the bell was whipped twelve times on his bare back while the timekeeper was asked to kneel down and raise his hands high up in the air throughout the duration of the assembly. Since that day the timekeeper never kept the bell on the window again. Instead he was keeping it on the ground near his feet. But like before whenever a teacher was not in the class, he would be fiddling with the tongue of the bell. One day he was pulling the tongue of the bell and it came off. He tried to stick the tongue back, but he could not. He became stricken with fear. For a long time he was holding the bell and the tongue in his hand not knowing what to do. What was he to tell my headmaster? Break-time came; there was no bell for the timekeeper to ring. My headmaster came to know why the timekeeper had not rang the bell for the pupils to go on break only to find the bell tongue severed from the bell.

'How did it happen?' my headmaster asked.

'It just fell off, sir,' said the timekeeper, avoiding my headmaster's face. My headmaster's eyes had a way of bringing out the truth from any pupil.

'Just like that?' my headmaster asked.

'Yes, sir.'

'I don't believe you,' said my headmaster. 'Even the leaf of a tree does not fall off just like that. The wind must pluck it. Class, what happened to the bell?' my headmaster turned on the class.

Every pupil looked at the other, but no one was ready to speak though they all knew how the timekeeper used to pull the tongue of the bell. Some of them had even warned him to desist from the habit, telling him the tongue could come off, but he refused to heed their warning. Yet, now no pupil was ready to tell my headmaster how the tongue came off lest he be accused of betraying a classmate.

'Will nobody in this class tell me what happened to the school bell?' my headmaster asked in a menacing voice.

Still nobody spoke.

'Fine,' said my headmaster. 'All of you kneel down until you can tell me what happened to the school bell.'

They all knelt down.

'You are going to remain on your knees until closing time unless you are honest enough to tell me what happened to the bell. What am I saying? The school now has no bell to be rung to close it; so it will not close until nightfall. We know time only by the school bell and since there is no bell now, nightfall would be what will tell us the school should close. So you are going to remain where you are till nightfall unless…'

On hearing this Musa one of the pupils in the timekeeper's class did not know when he raised his hand to speak.

'Yes, Musa what happened to the bell?' asked my headmaster.

'The timekeeper pulled off the tongue of the bell,' Musa said. 'He is in the habit of pulling it and we have warned him several times to desist from the habit, but he refused.'

'Why didn't you report him to me?' asked my headmaster.

Musa was now the accused and he could see the timekeeper and other classmates who thought he was a traitor nodding their heads happily. He could not answer my headmaster's query.

'Good boy, honest boy,' my headmaster said, cutting short Musa's agony. 'For telling the truth, Musa stand up,' he continued, looking at him with a rare tender look. 'The rest of you remain where you are, until your knees begin to advise your minds to tell the truth in all situations,' he turned on Musa's classmates, giving them a sweeping, hard look. Turning to Musa again, he said, 'I wonder why I did not make you a prefect.'

In front of the assembly that day, the timekeeper was whipped by my headmaster. Seeing the trouble the timekeeper often got into with my headmaster, when I was told his regret in not making Musa a prefect, I felt Musa was better off by my headmaster's indiscretion, if an indiscretion it was. Even the discipline prefect who had the privilege of beating pupils that were late to assembly in the morning exercised the power of his office under the constant fear of my headmaster. Two days after the timekeeper was punished for pulling off the tongue of the school bell, the discipline prefect came under the hammer of my headmaster for a discriminatory punishment he meted out to me when I along other pupils came late to assembly.

Chapter Eleven

Assembly and the Morning Dew

Eight o'clock in the morning was assembly time in Sarai Primary School. It meant a child who would trek four kilometres would have to leave home around seven in the morning. In the rainy season, whenever there was early morning rain or heavy dewfall, making the school assembly was always a difficult task. I did not care much about rain as I did about dew. Early morning rain was not frequent and if the rain began falling while we were still at home or its falling appeared imminent, our parents usually made us to remain at home until the rain was over. Then we would be chanting the common song my headmaster had taught us to chant to chase rain away:

Rain, rain, go away
Little children want to go to school
Come again another day.

Of course the rain rarely heeded this song and so we had to remain at home until it was over. But it was not the same thing with dew. Dew fell every day of the rainy season and no one would tell you to stay at home until grasses had shed off their dew no matter how heavy the dew fell the previous night or was falling in the morning.

On a night that there was a heavy dewfall, whoever had the misfortune of being the first to follow the path between Tyosa and Sarai the following morning, was certain to reach school drenched, particularly from his waist down. On such a morning, it was impossible to walk as fast as one ordinarily would because, often, one had to beat the grasses to shed off some of their dew on the ground if it was not to be shed on the person.

Bad as that was, it was better than being late to assembly. My headmaster had appointed a Discipline Prefect who seemed to have earned that office only on account of his wickedness. Every day he cordoned off those who were late at assembly and whipped them, often very cruelly, after the assembly.

The school assembly began with songs and parade, followed by prayer, homilies from my headmaster and announcement if there was any. Some days there was inspection of the pupils' uniform, fingernails and teeth by the health prefect before the final song that would take the pupils to their classes brought the assembly to an end. Mostly the first song that was sung on assembly was:

> I hear the bell
> It says to me
> Come, come, come, come to school.
> To school
> I hear the bell
> It says to me
> Come, come, come, come to school.

This song was always closely followed by:

> Punctuality and regularity is my motto
> Punctuality and regularity is my motto

The moment these songs were sung, the Discipline Prefect would cordon off those who had not joined the assembly before or during the songs. They were always packed together in a row behind the assembly where they remained until the assembly was over. The Discipline Prefect would then decide how many strokes of the cane he would give them and on which part of their bodies. In addition to flogging them, he might ask them to frog-jump or cut grass. My headmaster always took a keen interest in the type of punishment the Discipline Prefect meted out to late comers. He hated late coming and he was severe on late comers. But, even with his dislike for late coming, often he had to exercise a restraining influence on the Discipline Prefect's penchant for inflicting excessive punishment on late comers. He also made sure the Discipline Prefect meted out the same punishment on all late comers.

The Discipline Prefect my headmaster appointed when I was in primary one was a huge boy who no pupil could challenge or beat up. It was a deliberate choice. Even without the authority of his office, he could beat up anybody in the school in a fight. So he would not fear to deal with anybody who committed an offence. Already he carried authority in the muscles and sinews of his arms and the one given by the school only served to give legitimacy to what he was already capable of.

Two days after the timekeeper was punished by my headmaster for pulling off the tongue of the school bell, dew fell heavily through the night and the early part of the following morning. It was as if heaven was weeping for the whipping I will receive from the Discipline Prefect for coming late to assembly on this day.

I along three other pupils from Tyosa who like me dreaded dew, did not leave home early because of the dew. When we got within earshot of the school, the first thing we heard was:

> Punctuality and regularity is my motto
> Punctuality and regularity is my motto

By the time we reached the school, assembly proceedings had gone far and the Discipline Prefect, as usual, had already cordoned off late comers. Two of the pupils with me on seeing this from afar decided to hide behind thick bushes so as not to be seen by the Discipline Prefect or indeed other pupils. They would wait for the assembly to be over and would go and find somewhere to play until school was over. They dared not go home because their parents would want to know why they were not at school. They dared not go to their classes because their teachers would not only give them what the Discipline Prefect could not give them, but might drive them out of the class after whipping them. I so much liked school that I would rather receive the cane of the Discipline Prefect than sneaked into hiding. So I continued running to the school where I joined other late comers.

Like all late comers before us, we were standing behind the assembly waiting for the pleasure of the Discipline Prefect. Though we could hear and see the proceedings of the assembly as they wound themselves towards completion, we did not participate. Our minds were possessed more by the punishment the Discipline Prefect would mete out on us than getting involved in the assembly proceedings. As soon as the assembly was over, the Discipline Prefect walked towards us. There was menace in his walk and violence in the atmosphere he carried with him. The violence and menace that walked with him towards us were so sensible that I could feel them with my hand and so dense that I could lean on any of them. He held his cane in his right hand; striking the open palm of his left hand lightly with the cane and biting his lower lips in a manner that communicated the brewing of a sinister design. The picture he cut before all of us was that he was debating in the council of his mind the best kind of punishment he should inflict on us with maximum pain. We stood looking at him in trepidation. For quite sometime, he stood before us saying nothing. His head was raised up while his cane continued striking his open palm lightly. He seemed to want to torture us first by prolonging our anticipation of punishment before the punishment came. Eventually he looked down and his eyes fell on me. The moment he saw me, his countenance became more sinister. He did not like me and I knew it. I also knew why he did not like me.

Generally, the Discipline Prefect did not like brilliant pupils because he was not brilliant. He was appointed Discipline Prefect not because of his brains, but because of his brawn. Though I was in class one and he was in class six, he knew I was brilliant. He had heard how I was called to a senior class to recite the names of towns and villages to the shame of my half-brother lacking in brains like him. He obviously did not like that. How was he to know that one day I would not be called to his class for some other intellectual performance that would put him and his likes to shame? I had also earned his special hatred when I was indiscreet enough to laugh when he could not pronounce *social studies* correctly. Since then, he seemed to have marked me for destruction. But I had never given him the opportunity to vent his anger on me. Now I had given him the opportunity he so much needed and he seemed to be bursting with vengeance. Because of me, I presumed, he threw away the stick he was holding and brought out a rubber tube from his pocket. The tube no doubt inflicted more pain. He asked us to put out our open palms. He gave each person five strokes of the rubber on the open palm. But when he came to me, he would extend the rubber beyond my open palm to strike me on my forearm which was more painful. This he did perhaps to punish me for having the temerity to laugh at him; perhaps to discourage me from trying to be brilliant – a desire he might have a robust hope of its fulfilment given that I was still in class one and so could easily be imposed upon. Or he might have wished both to punish me and deter me from brilliance. On his last whip, which stung me more than the rest, I yelled out in pain and my headmaster came out of his office to know what was amiss. When I saw my headmaster, I cried louder than before.

'What is going on here?' my headmaster asked, coming to stand by us.

Before the Discipline Prefect could say anything, I cried, 'he is beating me differently from the way he is beating the others. He is beating them on their palms while he beats me on my forearm. I don't know why he hates me, sir. Sir, see my hand,' I said, extending my arm to my headmaster.

He looked at my forearm and saw the stripes left behind by the rubber tube and also checked the forearms of the other pupils the Discipline Prefect had already whipped, but saw nothing. He was enraged.

'What is the meaning of this?' my headmaster turned on the Discipline Prefect, showing my forearms with the rubber stripes on them.

The Discipline Prefect did not say anything. But guilt was written all over his face.

'I say what is the meaning of this?' my headmaster repeated in a more heated voice.

'Sorry sir,' the Discipline Prefect murmured, looking at the ground.

'That is not an answer to my question imbecile,' my headmaster bellowed.

The Discipline Prefect was now trembling with fear.

'What you have done calls for an assembly and there would be one to deal with it,' said my headmaster.

At the assembly which took place before the school closed that day, my headmaster called the Discipline Prefect to the front of the assembly. After telling the assembly the discriminatory way the Discipline Prefect whipped me that morning, he called me to the front of the assembly to know how many times I was whipped by the Discipline Prefect.

'Five times sir,' I said.

'Discipline Prefect, give me the rubber you used to whip him,' demanded my headmaster.

The Discipline Prefect handed over the rubber tube to him.

'Remove your dress and lie face down,' my headmaster commanded.

The Discipline Prefect removed his dress and lay down.

Using the rubber tube the Discipline Prefect used to whip me and other late comers, my headmaster whipped the Discipline Prefect on his bare back five times. Writhing in pain, the Discipline Prefect stood up when my headmaster was through. Before my eyes, he now looked so abject that I wondered if he would find dignity again.

'Now listen to me,' my headmaster said to the Discipline Prefect. 'I did not make you Discipline Prefect to discriminate against anybody, but to be fair to everyone. You were appointed to be an agent of justice not a witch-hunter, imbecile,' he said and paused for a while before he continued. 'There is only one thing that counts in this life and that thing is justice. Even God does not count that much. All the strife in the world today is because of injustice. If justice returns to the world today, peace would return. All the hunger in the world today is because of injustice. If justice returns, food will return. All the disease afflicting the world today is because of injustice. If justice returns, health will return. Of course, you are an idiot and so cannot understand what I am saying. But I know there is one thing even an idiot like you will not fail to understand. If ever something like this happens again I will not only remove you as Discipline Prefect, but dismiss you from the school. Of course, I know dismissal from the school will not mean much to you since you don't seem to have learned anything all the years you have been here; but removal from the office of Discipline Prefect I know will hurt you than anything. So I will not even dismiss you from the school. I will rather leave you here to suffer the boos and jeers of your victims without the power to deal with any. That itself would be some form of justice.'

As my headmaster berated the Discipline Prefect, I wondered why the assembly could not take place after the school. That might take care of pupils who sometimes ran home before the school's closure time. But the timekeeper only rang his bell for pupils to come to assembly in the morning. If his bell called pupils to assembly at some other time, it must be on the instruction of my headmaster. The voice and eyes of my headmaster were everywhere. In the case of his eyes, they were frighteningly everywhere – even on our teeth. Thinking of the eyes of my headmaster on our teeth, it never occurred to me his eyes would indeed visit our teeth the following day to the chagrin of most of us, including the health prefect.

Chapter Twelve

Show Me Your Teeth

The following day, we set out for school from our village Tyosa a little earlier than usual. The previous night there was less dewfall. But even with this, most of us dreaded going into the bush to cut chewing sticks to brush their teeth. Luckily for us, the *sunsom* shrub which was the shrub we often cut our chewing sticks from was always by the wayside so that we did not have to enter the bush to get our chewing sticks. Moving on the small path to the school, a pupil could cut a chewing stick from the shrub without having to take a step out of the path into the bush.

We were seven pupils on the path and I was second to the last person on the line. Behind me was Ateh who we had nicknamed *Nahiu*, meaning: one whose mouth smells. Ateh's teeth were always so dirty that often when he laughed, blood would be seen coming out of the crevices of his teeth. When he bit a piece of yam, he was likely to leave little bloodstains on the piece still in his hand. His mouth was always full of foul saliva and stank like an open latrine. He was popularly called *Nahiu* by all the pupils of our class.

There were three places in the human body that evil spirits were said to live: the mouth, the stomach and the head. In the mouth and the stomach, they found food. In the head they influence the thoughts of a man. When a man became mad people said the evil spirits in his head were up in arms against him. Because spirits lived in the mouth and the stomach, when a man was hungry, he would say *those in the stomach have started demanding their tax,* which means the spirits of the stomach were asking for food.

The spirits living in in Ateh's mouth were said to be excreting and urinating in his mouth instead of going out for their conveniences. That was why his mouth was always smelling and full of foul saliva.

Today Ateh was walking behind me. None of us in the group of seven walking on the path was yet to cut a chewing stick to start brushing his mouth – a ritual we performed everyday on our way to school. It was perhaps because the day was not a personal hygiene inspection day. But as we moved close to river Yatuk, the third boy from the front of our little line stopped walking and took hold of the twig of a *sunsom* shrub by the wayside and began twisting it so as to severe it from the stock. The boy walking behind him sidestepped him and walked on. But the boy I walked behind stopped by the same shrub and began twisting another twig. I also stopped by the same shrub to do the same thing. But Ateh walked past us.

As I twisted the twig I wanted to use as chewing stick, I could see a vulture perched on an *alyiet* tree not far away. My mind immediately went to what my headmaster always told us about the vulture, the pig and the hyena.

'Food, I mean too much food, as far as I am concerned is not a friend,' my headmaster would say. 'Look at the pig, the vulture and the hyena. Food has messed them up. Sometimes the hyena is wounded or killed because of its reckless search for food. Too much food has made the hyena a fool. The pig is a roaming stomach without a head. The pig speaks through the nose because the mouth is too full to speak. It cannot even raise its head so as not to miss out on any food. Sometimes it is crushed by fast moving vehicles because its ears listen only to the command of its stomach. My boys,' he would say, his voice rising to a pitch, 'don't risk your heads to please your stomachs. Don't allow your stomach to drag your name in mud. The vulture perches with hunched shoulders, a sunken neck and bleary eyes, almost lifeless watching out for food. The vulture is lifeless because of what it eats. While other birds screech and shriek, the vulture hisses and grunts. Who is the vulture hissing at? It must be at life since instead of eating what has life, the vulture is eating only what has death in it. Grunting means the mouth is full and so talking must be through the nose. What can the mouth of the vulture be full of? It must be death since it is stuffing only carrion into its gizzard. When the vulture belches, it belches only death through its nostrils, since that is the only thing it eats.'

As I thought of what my headmaster used to say about the vulture and its fellow gluttons, I could see the boy who first stopped by the shrub I was standing by had severed his twig from the stock we were cutting our chewing sticks from and was beginning to peel off the bark of the chewing stick. That was the good thing about *sunsom* shrub. Its twig might be difficult to sever from the shrub, it was so easy to defoliate. Its bark came off the stem in a rope form. This made the *sunsom* shrub a ready source of ropes to tie firewood or any other forest growth.

After defoliating the chewing stick and wringing off the upper part of the stick which he did not need, the boy who first stopped to get a chewing stick moved on. By that time I and the other boy had severed our own twigs from the stock and were peeling off the bark. Not far away from where we were, we could see other boys severing twigs from different *sunsom* shrubs. That was always the case with us. Once one of us decided to get a chewing stick to brush his teeth, all of us would do the same thing.

I walked past Ateh. He was still twisting and pulling at the twig he was trying to severe from a *sunsom* shrub. All other boys had finished severing theirs and were defoliating them. I suspected that Ateh had deliberately refused to sever his twig from the stock so that he would bring up the rear again. My suspicion was confirmed when as soon as I walked past him, the twig he was severing came off from the stock and he began to peel off its bark.

The chewing stick I cut was too hard for my teeth. After attempting to chew it from both ends to a brush without much success, I began using the little brush my chewing had produced to brush my teeth. But that did not mean the end of my chewing of the stick. Usually brushing and chewing of the stick intermingled. One moment the stick was chewed; the next moment it was used to brush the teeth only to be chewed again. As I chewed and brushed my teeth with the chewing stick, I spat out the saliva the chewing stick had stimulated in my mouth. Other pupils were doing the same thing.

Behind me Ateh was also chewing his stick. But I could see he was doing little brushing, may be because of the fear of blood that would gush out of his gums if he exerted too much pressure on them. Whenever he was brushing his teeth on our way to school in the morning, he tried to hide what he was doing from other pupils. That was why he always wanted to walk behind so that no one would see him brushing his teeth and see the blood such activity drew from his gums. Once I turned to see him spat saliva out of his mouth. It was full of blood. It seemed the chewing stick instead of stimulating saliva in his mouth stimulated blood. The spirits in his mouth must be very angry today and that was why his gums were bringing out so much blood.

After brushing my teeth for sometimes with the chewing stick, I threw it away into the bush. By this time we were almost in river Yatuk. As I was entering the river, I heard a little swishing sound and I looked back to see Ateh's chewing stick that had just fallen into the bush where he had thrown it. It was full of blood. Like other pupils, I entered the river and rinsed my mouth.

We got to school way off the time for assembly and went to play. When the bell for assembly rang, we ran to line up. After the first song, to our surprise my headmaster followed by the health prefect began a personal hygiene spot check. None of us was expecting this inspection and so no one came prepared for it. The worse thing was that the inspection was by my headmaster instead of the health prefect who usually carried out the inspection. That was my headmaster. He was a man none of us could predict.

My headmaster was in front followed by the health prefect. There were three principal parts of a pupil's body that were inspected: teeth, fingernails and uniform. Whichever pupil was found wanting in any of these areas, my headmaster would ask him to stretch out the back of his palm with the fingers curled up into the fists of a leper, which perhaps in the mind of my headmaster the owner of the hand failing to live by the simple rules of personal hygiene was. He would rap his ruler on the knuckles, his eyeballs rolling in their sockets like a dice on a Ludo plate. It was always a very painful thing, particularly on a cold morning. When the ruler was rapped on a pupil's knuckles, he would always snatch in searing pain the hand that was rapped, flexing it in the air for some relief.

Now my headmaster was inspecting my line. 'Show me your teeth,' he said to the boy in front of me.

The boy bared his teeth at my headmaster.

'Not so clean,' said my headmaster.

My heart sank. I knew the boy to be a very neat boy. If my headmaster was saying his teeth were not clean enough, I wondered what he would say or do to me; for the boy was better than me in personal hygiene. I was more worried because that day I did not brush my teeth with the chewing stick the way I used to. Now I was regretting the hasty way I threw away the chewing stick. But if my headmaster found my teeth not to be clean, I wondered what he would do to Ateh four pupils behind me.

Soon my headmaster was standing before me, his eyes boring into my bared teeth and whiffs of hot air from his nostrils fanning my face.

'Your teeth are dirty,' he said in a flush of displeasure. 'What is the matter? Every child's mouth still carries what he ate five days ago. This is unacceptable. But a fish always starts decaying from the head.' Saying this, he turned on the health prefect following him and to every pupil's shock, asked him to show him his teeth. This had never happened before. The health prefect who had the privilege of inspecting others was now the subject of inspection. It was unthinkable. But with my headmaster anything was possible.

The health prefect bared his teeth to the amazement and happiness of all the pupils in the assembly.

My headmaster rolled his eyes over his teeth and seemed not to like what he was seeing. 'You see what I mean,' he said, loudly to the hearing of everyone in the assembly. 'Health prefect, you are not much better than the other pupils. You have to improve your own personal hygiene. Until you do so, we have no right inspecting other pupils.' Saying this, he turned and walked back to the small veranda in front of the assembly.

Behind me, I could see Ateh smiling.

We began singing the song we usually sang to mark the end of assembly before marching off into our various classes:

> We go to our classes with clean hearts and faces
> To pay great attention to what we are taught.
> Or else we shall never be happy and clever
> For learning is better than silver and gold.

Midway into our singing a hush fell over the assembly. My headmaster was speaking: 'How can we go into our classes with clean hearts and faces when every pupil's mouth is smelling and goo is in the eyelids of every pupil?' my headmaster's voice boomed through the Assembly. 'More like going to our classes with dirty hearts and faces,' he continued, his eyeballs flaming fire. 'With dirty hearts and faces, we can pay no attention to what we are taught and so would be unhappy and stupid.   How can we go into our classes with clean hearts and faces without punishing the health prefect and every child that came dirty to school today?' As he spoke, he began coming down the veranda he had earlier walked up. He was coming down to punish the health prefect and continue his inspection where he stopped.

My heart sank. Behind me, a cloud of sadness hung over Ateh's face.

Chapter Thirteen

The Old Woman that will not Die

Near our school, there was an old locust bean tree called *the old woman that would not die.* It was a low-lying tree that reminded people of an old woman stooping on her walking stick. From oral tradition, the tree was a very old tree. So it was called *the old woman that would not die.*

My headmaster was fond of *the old woman that would not die.* He always took us there for story telling and songs. He said the tree inspired him to tell us good stories and sing us good songs. There was a day he joked that the stories he told us were not told by him, but by *the old woman that would not die.* In the innocence of childhood, I almost believed him because, almost all the stories I knew before coming to the school, were told to me by my grandmother – an old woman.

When we went to the tree for a story telling class, we all sat on the trunk of the low-lying tree together with my headmaster. Before he told us a story, he would first sing a melodious song that was to some of us some sort of appetizer for the stories he would tell.

On the day my headmaster punished the health prefect and other pupils for coming to school dirty, we went with my headmaster to *the old woman that would not die* for a story telling class. Sitting on *the old woman that would not die* on this day, my headmaster sang us this song:

> I have no father in this world
> I have no mother in this world
> I have no brother in this world
> I have no sister in this world

I sat in the night
When the moon was so bright
At the bank of river Niger
At the bank of river Niger
At the bank of river Niger
I sat in the night
When the moon was so bright
At the bank of river Niger.

When singing, my headmaster had such a melodious voice. He was said to be the choirmaster of his church when he was much younger. As choirmaster, he was such a gifted singer that he composed his own songs. But now, my headmaster hardly attended church. He said the worldly attitudes of the pastors had driven him away from the church.

As he sang this song on *the old woman that would not die*, tears came to my eyes and on his third round of singing the song, I was singing it with him. So were other pupils of my class. As we sang, I was looking at *the old woman that will not die*. Towards where the tree forked into branches, there was an indentation that had the shape of a mouth. The tree seemed to be singing with us through its mouth.

After the song, he told us this story:

In Mayat three worlds away from Sarai, lived five girls with their mothers. Everyday the girls would go to the forest to pick *luu* – a sweet forest fruit. All the girls except Kulak would bring some of their fruits to their mothers. One day Kulak's fiancй living in a far away village died and Kulak and her mates were supposed to attend his funeral ceremony. The girls needed good wrappers to tie to the funeral ceremony. All the girls' mothers gave their wrappers to their daughters except Kulak's mother. She said she would only give her wrapper to Kulak if the girl went back to the forest and brought her *luu*. Desperate, Kulak left for the forest to get *luu* for her mother. Meanwhile her friends with wrappers departed for the funeral ceremony.

When Kulak got to the forest, she went to the *aluu* tree where she and her friends usually picked the fruits that had fallen on the ground. But there was no *luu* on the ground. All the *luu* had climbed up the tree. She started begging the *aluu* tree to shed off its fruits for her to take to her mother. In a Hausa song she would tell the tree what she needed and the tree would ask her why:

Dinya, dinya ki yi in kwashe
Ki kwashe ki yi me da shi?
In kwashe in baa uwa na
Uwanki ta yi me da shi
Uwana ta bani zani
Zani ki yi me da shi?
Zani in tafi kuka
Kuka na wanene?
Kuka na Dogara ne
Dogara ya mutu asha!

The tree told her it would not shed its fruits until she brought cow dung and rubbed about it. She went to a herd of cows and sang the same song. But the cows said they would not give their dung until she brought grasses to them. She went to a field of grasses, but the grasses asked for water. It was only water that surrendered to her without a demand. She carried the water to the grasses which now surrendered to her. She carried the grasses to the cows which gave her their dung. She carried the dung and rubbed about the tree which now gave her the *luu*. She carried the fruits to her mother who gave her the wrapper. By then it was already evening. But she was bent on attending the funeral ceremony of her fiancй. So she set out for his village. She got to the village at sunset to find the funeral was over. Frustrated and embarrassed, she headed back home. Very soon it was night. Hyenas, tigers and snakes started chasing her. She ran home pursued by these wild animals. When she got home, every door was locked because everyone had gone to sleep. She ran to her mother's room crying to be led in:

Nma nang eeeh
Jang jang jang
Iya nang eeh
Jang jang jang
Kai nyip nang avokah
Jang jang jang
Kyang a yit na yah nang oo
Jang jang jang
Ba nyuih ba chui oo
Jang jang jang

The mother refused to open her door and she ran to her father's room and sang the same song. Her father took pity on her and opened the door for her. She entered and he closed the door against the wild animals that were chasing her.

'Once upon a time,' my headmaster began another story with only a momentary pause after the first story, 'there lived an old tortoise in a big forest. 'The tortoise was a very dishonest and treacherous animal. The forest had paths that animals followed to the river, to neighbouring and far villages and to their farms and homes. But the old tortoise never followed any of these paths. When going to the river or another village, the old tortoise would not follow the known path to the river or the village, but would instead take to the bush. Many animals wondered why the tortoise would not follow the paths other animals followed, but chose to be a bushwhacker. However, the few animals that knew the old tortoise well knew why he would not follow the beaten paths. The old tortoise was a thief. He stole crops and other valuables of the animals. If he followed a path, he would be seen or he would meet someone on the path with the stolen property. But if he sneaked through the mesh of the forest, no one saw him and he would meet no one.

Alone in the bush, the old tortoise used to say, 'a path is like a tail behind and a beard in front that others can use to tie you to a tree and flog you. I have neither tail nor beard. Those who follow paths leave footprints behind and I aspire to walk like a shadow leaving no traces of my goings and comings for anyone to see. Besides, the bush connects me faster with my destinations than the paths.'

One day the old tortoise stole yam from the rabbit's farm and was hurrying home with his loot before nightfall. Rain clouds were also brimming in the sky and there was nothing the old tortoise feared like rain. As he walked home through the bush as he was wont to, his left leg slipped into a hole he could not see because of the forest growth that covered it. He pulled at his leg, but the leg would not come out of the hole. It was as if there was another animal inside the hole holding onto his leg. 'I am done for,' cried the old tortoise. 'I am not a shadow after all, but an old tortoise with a leg that can be held. Perhaps, it is better to leave footprints on the path than a leg in a hole.'

After my headmaster told us this story, he sang songs that in later years I saw as his desserts:

Oh I couldn't hear nobody pray
Oh I couldn't hear nobody pray
When I went down yonder by myself
I couldn't hear nobody pray.
In the valley
I couldn't hear nobody pray,
On my knees
I couldn't hear nobody
Oh I couldn't hear nobody pray
Oh I couldn't hear nobody pray
When I went down yonder by myself
I couldn't hear nobody pray.

Na ji murya daga sama

Bani mutane na
Fir'auna, Fir'auna
Ka bani mutane na:

Pharaoh Pharaoh
The king of Egypt
Pharaoh pharaoh
Pharaoh let my people go.

Like *the old woman that would not die*, the stories my
headmaster told us on that tree and the songs he sang for us would
never die in me.

Chapter Fourteen

The Dust Exercise Book

Most of primary one, the dust of the school arena was our exercise book. It was on the dust we did our English, arithmetic, social studies and drawing, and our teacher marked our tests for us there, and we went home without anything to show our parents whether we were doing well at school or not. Serious and brilliant pupils had nothing to be proud of and unserious and dull pupils had nothing to worry or be ashamed of because both success and failure were left behind in the dust of the school arena. Even in the first term of class one, I was doing very well in English and social studies. My problem was with arithmetic. I just did not seem to be able to add, subtract, divide or multiply numbers accurately. But as my exercise book was the dust of the school arena, I had nothing to worry about because I always left my failure behind me in the school.

My headmaster taught us most of class one. He would write out his questions on the blackboard placed against the wall of the class and the pupils would write out their answers on the dust of the school. Usually the time allowed for answering his questions was five minutes. After the five minutes, he would walk from pupil to pupil marking the answers.

That we started learning by writing on dust was partly because exercise books were not readily available and partly because my headmaster insisted that was the best way to proceed. We were country children used to dust. We played with it at home in various forms: Sometimes we used it to prepare meals the way we saw our mothers prepare meals with grounded millet or guinea corn. Sometimes we used dust to play *kodi*. Sometimes we used clay which is like dust to make pots and other household utensils. Every rainy season our parents turned up the earth to plant crops and we played with the turned-up earth. We smashed anthills to behold the ants and play with the ruins of the anthill. We went to the river and played on the sand of the river. We were born into dust and raised up on dust. So we were very intimate with dust.

My headmaster believed in starting from the familiar to the unfamiliar. The law of parsimony he called it. He believed in evolution not revolution. He said since our hands were already used to dust, we should start writing with dust using our fingers which were already used to dust. When our fingers could scrawl something legible on dust, they could be relied on more to hold a pencil and scrawl something legible on paper. This in itself would reduce waste.

There was a lot of dust in the school arena and so no pupil lacked dust to write on. Even in the rainy season, there was always sand on which to write unless rain fell that day, in which case the mud left behind by the rain was as good a slate for writing.

During our dust writing exercises, each child would scoop in front of him a heap of dust which he would spread out to produce a flat surface suitable for writing. During our first two weeks in the school, our writings were like tracks of decapitated earthworms. Not much sense could be made of them. But by the third week, some of us had begun to acquire proficiency that introduced legibility and intelligence into what hitherto was a poor imitation of writing.

On the sixth week, my headmaster came to mark my arithmetic on the dust I had written it. He had given us five sums and was going from pupil to pupil to mark what we had written. When he got to me, he took a look at what I had written and began to cancel them one after the other. After he had cancelled the first three sums, I felt like starting a wind to obliterate the remaining knowing they would suffer the same fate.

'What is the matter with you, Nto?' asked my headmaster. 'You are so good in English and social studies, yet so poor in arithmetic. 'Are you sure you pay the same attention to arithmetic that you pay to other subjects?'

I was surprised how my headmaster was able to know I did not pay the same attention to arithmetic that I paid to other subjects. Whenever arithmetic was being taught, my mind was always thinking of something else. I could not even see the sense in learning a subject that would not enable me read stories my headmaster used to read to us or that would not help me write a letter. When my father wanted to write a letter, it was my elder brother who then was in primary six that wrote for him. Very soon he would complete his primary school and go to secondary school. I wanted to replace him as my father's letter-writer. So I gave all my attention to knowing how to read and write alphabets, not numbers. This arithmetic I had just failed, my mind was scarcely in it when I was solving the sums we were given. Yet, I was not happy when I failed the test. I was so unhappy that when my headmaster asked me why I was doing so badly in arithmetic, I felt like crying. Later, I found out that my feelings were not strange. Even unserious pupils always wanted to pass their examinations. Even unserious pupils like teachers who could teach well. All hunters want to kill games whether they are good or bad hunters.

'I am sorry sir,' I said to my headmaster.

'Be more serious with your arithmetic,' said my headmaster. 'Very soon you will start writing on exercise books. How would you like your exercise book on arithmetic to be full of zeros?'

This sank into my mind than anything else. Now I could leave my failure in the dust of the school and go back home without fear of anyone seeing that I was such a bad pupil in arithmetic. Not so when we begin writing on exercise books. Then I would have to carry my failure with me or be replacing exercise books everyday. Where would I find the money to be buying the exercise books daily? Even if I could buy them, I would still have to explain why my exercise book on arithmetic was always blank. If my failure in arithmetic was reflected on an exercise book, I would lose my rating as a brilliant pupil among my friends and siblings. I would do anything to avoid a fall in my reputation. There was another reason I had to do well in arithmetic. On vacation day, pupils who did well in all subjects were called by my headmaster to the front of the assembly for commendation. Those who performed poorly in their subjects were also called by my headmaster for rebuke. The school assembly was in many ways a horror chamber for erring and unserious pupils though it might be a pleasure park to my headmaster.

From the day my headmaster wondered why I was so bad in arithmetic, I took the subject more seriously and was surprised by the result. I took first position in primary one. Even now, I don't know how I came to earn that position. The first day I knew I took first position, I was elated. But, when I got home, it was a lambaste I got from my uncle. I met him on my way home and in the excitement I was, I told him I had been informed I took first position in my class. My uncle was disappointed that all I could get in a class of forty three pupils was ONE when more brilliant children took as much as THIRTY-SIX and even FORTY-ONE. He lambasted me and I went home crying and confused.

At home, my father laughed when he learned of my uncle's understanding of first position. He assured me that contrary to my uncle's opinion, I was in fact brilliant. I was happy again. The fearful eyes of my headmaster would look kindly upon me on vacation day when I would be called to the front of the assembly for honour.

Chapter Fifteen

Big Heads, Big Stomachs, Stupid Heads

In our year three in the primary school, those of us who were brilliant in class were known and those who were dull were also known. The dull ones my headmaster called big heads, big stomachs and stupid heads.

Ayuba was a boy in my class with a very big head. His head was so big that it looked like an earthen pot on top of his neck. Whenever he walked, his head shot forward and seemed to propel him forward as much as his legs. It was well it was forward the gravity of his head lay. If it were backward, walking would have been near impossible with him because then while his legs would be walking him forward, his head would be walking him backward. That would be a sort of tug-of-war that would have been quite crippling and torturous to Ayuba. Being moved forward by two propellers – his head as his legs, Ayuba wobbled in his walk. This made us to call him *Chicken Scare*. Wobbling as he did, he was more liable to scare away chickens than the normal person.

Chicken Scare was a very dull pupil. He had no head for any subject though he had a big head that recommended big brain. My headmaster said in place of the milk that should be in *Chicken Scare*'s coco, there was mucus. He called him cocoyam head on account of his blinking stupidity. The head of a cocoyam is always bigger than the lobes that grow out of it. But the little lobes are tastier and therefore are liked more. *Chicken Scare* had no friend in the school and so walked mostly alone.

In addition to being dull in class, *Chicken Scare* was a glutton. Some pupils said chickens ran away from him not because of his wobbling walk, but because they knew he could eat all of them at once. In an eating competition, *Chicken Scare* ate three big tubers of yam alone and drank nearly a basin of water. He came first in that competition. The pupil that was a distant second to him ate only a tuber and a half. Even with all the yams in his stomach, his belly did not seem to bulge in a very significant way. Some pupils joked that much of the yam he ate went to his head instead of his stomach. Others carried the joke further by saying that since his head was always empty, it was only proper some of the yams should take residence there. These jokes acquired an embarrassing authority when two weeks after the yam eating competition, my headmaster in a drawing class asked us to draw an elephant and *Chicken Scare* drew what looked like a tuber of yam.

I had never seen my headmaster laughed like that. 'Wonderful, Good God!' he kept exclaiming. Who would have thought it was true when the joke was being bandied? Wonderful!' He took *Chicken Scare*'s book from him and asked him to follow him to the front of the class.

In front of the class, he turned the inside of *Chicken Scare*'s drawing book to face the class with the index finger of his right hand on what *Chicken Scare* had drawn.

Chicken Scare stood before the class chewing his lips. That was his well known habit. Some pupils said he was so used to eating food that if there was nothing for him to eat, he ate his lips.

'Class, does this look like an elephant to you?' asked my headmaster.

Nearly the whole class shouted, 'no!'

'What does this drawing look like or reminds you of?'

The class answered almost in unison, 'a tuber of yam.'

My headmaster dropped the drawing book on the teacher's table and once more reeled with laughter. When he finished laughing, he picked up the drawing book again and asked, 'specifically can you remember any tuber of yam you have ever seen that this drawing reminds you of?'

There was no immediate reply.

'Think well,' my headmaster urged us.

Just when he thought no one would give him the answer he desired, a boy sitting two rows in front of me raised his hand and my headmaster said, 'yes, you.'

'It reminds me of one of the tubers of yam Ayuba ate during the eating competition,' the boy said.

Almost everybody in the class was laughing now.

'You are a big wonder that requires study,' my headmaster said, turning on *Chicken Scare* after a good laugh. 'So the tubers of yam you ate actually went to your head, not to your stomach,' he said looking at *Chicken Scare* in utter amazement. 'Class, listen to me,' he said addressing the class. 'Food, too much food I mean, is not a friend to the brain. I don't even think it is a friend to the stomach. I have never met anyone who is a glutton and intelligent at the same time. It is not for nothing the head where the brain is has been placed over the stomach. If the stomach were over the head, it would have been a bad influence on the head. Look at animals in whom the head and the stomach are at the same level and you will understand why they are not as intelligent as man. Even among animals, the monkey which occasionally walked upright placing its head over its stomach is more intelligent. It is also not for nothing that the head and the stomach are far apart. If they live too close, there would be too much folly in the world. While hunger tends to excite intelligence, food tends to excite folly. Remember the story of the rich fool in the Bible. It was after he had eaten to surfeit that he started talking foolishly of building many barns to store his grains. Food crowds out thought as much as night crowds out light. It was not for nothing that Jesus Christ was at his finest in thought after fasting forty days and forty nights. It was not for nothing that he urged his disciples to go to places of mourning instead of feasting places.' He paused in his speech and looked at *Chicken Scare* again in wonder then continued. 'Cocoyam head!' he exclaimed; 'your stupidity stinks. Tending more to the entrails of the pot, you tend not the entrails of the head. Paying taxes only to the hyenas of the stomach, you pay no tax to the hares of the head. Watering the gardens of the stomach, you stoke not the fire in the head. Though I can neither understand the chemistry nor the biology of your stupidity, I can see its physics. Your stupidity sits on your forehead with an eagle feather,' he concluded and waved him away.

Just as *Chicken Scare* was about taking his seat, the boy sitting close to him said something to him in Tyap which unfortunately for him my headmaster heard. That was something about my headmaster. He had ears that could hear the grass grow and the footsteps of the air. Among the Atyap people, such ears were called gossiping ears because only a gossip needs to hear everything. But no one could call the ears of my headmaster gossiping ears because he was headmaster. His were rather keen ears.

'You who spoke vernacular, come here,' said my headmaster, his big eyeballs leaning out of their sockets to wave fear at us.

The pupil who spoke in Tyap came out to the front of the class where my headmaster was.

'Why did you speak in your mother tongue here?' asked my headmaster in such a tone that suggested he held Tyap in contempt. But because he himself was an Atyap man, the vexation his tone would have carried was lost in an unconscious folk-feeling: *after all he is one of us.* In my village, there were native doctors who used horns of rams and goats to remove poison and pain from human bodies. Folk-feelings were a native doctor's horn that removed the sting of insults. A man may insult his own son without either of them suffering offence. But if the same insult on his son were by another person, a quarrel or even a fight would erupt.

To return to my headmaster's anger against the pupil that spoke Tyap to *Chicken Scare* in class, 'Empty head,' he bellowed, 'have you forgotten the vernacular rule? For speaking vernacular in class before me, in addition to the fine you must pay, kneel down on those pebbles until break-time,' he said indicating a row of pebbles that were placed in each class for this purpose. The pupil went and knelt down on the pebbles and raised his hands in the air.

Chapter Sixteen

The Vernacular Rule

For pupils from primary three to six, my headmaster established an inflexible rule against speaking in vernacular. All pupils at this level must speak only English in the school. A breach of this rule attracted a fine of three kobo.

Vernacular is like *burukutu*, my headmaster would say, baring his eyeballs at us. 'It affects your mind; flee from it. Like *burukutu*, vernacular is bad for your soul. I may not think too highly of the Christian faith because of the conduct of people who called themselves Christians but behaved like devilians; but I think highly of the English language. By the way, the Christian faith and the English language are not synonymous. But English is synonymous with knowledge and vernacular synonymous with ignorance. English is light; vernacular is darkness. The children of light are locked in mortal conflict with the children of darkness.'

The way my headmaster spoke of English made me think there was no illiterate English man or even an ignorant one. The glorious terms he spoke of English were the glorious terms the pastor of my church spoke of Jerusalem. He spoke of Jerusalem in such heavenly terms that I never thought it was a city on earth. I was therefore quite surprised some years later when I saw Jerusalem in the world map and heard of pilgrimage to Jerusalem.

'The world I see ahead of you understands only English,' my headmaster would say. 'If you cannot speak that language well, the world will not only spit at you, it will spit you out. But if you can speak English well, the world has no choice but to carry you on its back the way women carry their infants. You know in the church they say halleluiah is our heavenly language. On earth here English is the language. Those who can speak and write it well will find peace on earth and I believe in heaven wherever heaven is. For, as it is on earth, it is in heaven. If you are selling firewood here, you are likely to sell firewood in heaven. All of us must read the scriptures with four eyes and two heads.

'You have not only to speak in English, but to think only in English when you are in this school. When you go back home, you can think and speak in your vernacular. It is from what the mind thinks that the mouth speaketh. If you must laugh in this school, laugh only in English. If you must cry, cry only in English.'

I, more than most of my classmates, took my headmaster serious on how bad vernacular was and tried not to speak Tyap even at home. I later came to feel I was able to speak English better than my classmates because I heeded the vernacular rule of my headmaster more.

The vernacular rule was the most dreaded rule to the pupil who was the discipline prefect when I was in primary three. When he took it out on late comers, this rule took it out on him. Because of the rule, he rarely spoke in school. If he must speak, he must speak in English like any other pupil in his class. If he spoke English, people laughed at him because it would be bad English. If he spoke vernacular and was caught, he had to pay the fine of three kobo. Faced with these two equally unpleasant options, he chose to be silent during school hours. But some pupils, particularly those he flogged for late coming would follow him around the school trying to draw him into a conversation. But he would not speak. When he refused to talk, some reckless pupils among them would start taunting him all in a bit to force him to talk. One of these pupils who used to taunt him was severely beaten by the discipline prefect when he went beyond taunting to poking him with a stick on his ribs. The discipline prefect without uttering a word grabbed him by his collar and beat him silly. He cried and went to report the discipline prefect to my headmaster.

'Why did he beat you?' my headmaster asked.

'Because he spoke vernacular and I threatened to report him to you,' said the pupil.

'Did you threaten to report him or meant to report him to me?'

'I meant to report him to you, sir.'

'Go and call him.'

The pupil ran and called the discipline prefect.

'Did you beat him?' my headmaster asked.

'*Yet*,' the discipline prefect answered.

'Why did you beat him?' This question called for a long explanation and the discipline prefect dreaded to answer it.

'Am I speaking to a stone?' shouted my headmaster.

'*Jit boy laugh me and choke hit luler in my rif, sing I beat hyim,*' said the discipline prefect, sweat breaking out on his forehead from the stress of having to speak in English.

Both my headmaster and the pupil laughed.

'You are in your final year and you are speaking this kind of English?' asked my headmaster. 'My boy, you are a major embarrassment. Already I can see the spit of the world on your face. You will graduate from this school and go out there to give us a bad name that we did not teach you well. No way. God knows I did my best. I will rather endorse on your certificate that we did our best to teach you, but you refused to learn because your head is filled with cow dung. Do you know something?' he asked the discipline prefect.

The discipline prefect shook his head.

'For seeds to germinate and grow into crops it is not enough that soils are fertile; the seeds must be fertile seeds. In fact, the land may be barren, but it would be fertilized by fertile seeds. If you have any doubt of this, look at the barren and desert land of Israel. See the oasis and fertile garden the fertile seed that is the mind of the Israeli has turned it into. The greatness of Israel as a nation lies in the greatness of the head of the Israeli than on any promised land flowing with milk and honey. If any land is flowing with milk and honey, it is the head of the Israeli and not the barren land of the Judean desert.

'On the other hand, you may have a fertile land, but if seeds planted on it are infertile, nothing good will come out of the labour because unlike fertile seeds, fertile lands cannot fertilize infertile seeds. If you have any doubt of this, look at Nigeria your country. The land is fertile, but the seeds are rotten and you can see the mess the rotten seeds have reduced the fertile land to. To graduate a brilliant pupil, it is not enough that this is a good school where pupils are well taught. The pupil himself must have some milk in his coco.'

From the expression on his face, it was clear the discipline prefect did not understand much of what my headmaster had said; neither did most of the pupils who listened to him.

'You, why were you poking him in the ribs?' my headmaster turned on the mischievous pupil, rather dramatically.

'Sir, I swear I did not poke at his ribs. I only said I will report him to you when I heard him speaking vernacular,' the pupil said, avoiding the eyes of my headmaster.

'I don't believe you,' said my headmaster. 'I rather believe him. 'I know you as a troublemaker. Now let me tell you what my father used to tell me: If a man is always in the forefront of battles, it would seem as if he has a mission to fulfil in the land of the dead. Do you have such a mission?' he asked, baring his eyeballs at the pupil who cringed from him.

'Because he cannot speak English, you went to court his trouble, is that not it? It is a good thing you are brilliant in class and speak good English. But don't use your brilliance to taunt those who are not. You had better advise your pride and thirst for trouble. If not, in addition to the swollen face you now wear, you may have a broken limb to nurse very soon. Let me tell you this story, my boy. Perhaps it would help you refrain from pride and wooing trouble, which by the way is not a maiden but an old prostitute.

'Once upon a time in Langson country there lived a monkey who was very intelligent. In fact he was considered more intelligent than all other animals. In the beginning, the monkey was humble and very pleasant to other animals. The story of his intelligence and humility travelled so far that it got into the ears of the lion who was the king of Langson country. The lion called the monkey to his palace and was so impressed by the monkey's intelligence and humility. But he was more impressed by the monkey's humility. To have this intelligence and be this humble was to the lion a very admirable thing. But the monkey thought all the admiration the lion had for him was because of his intelligence. The easiest thing my boy is that you can be intelligent and stupid at the same time. When the monkey was leaving the lion's palace, the hog, the giraffe and the jackal – courtiers in the lion's palace, followed him with their flutes singing songs in praise of his intellect. While the other animals had no evil motive in their praise, the jackal intended to destroy the monkey by his praise. Before the monkey came, he was considered the wisest animal in the lion's palace. What if the lion decides to make the monkey one of his courtiers? That would mean the end of his reign as the wisest counsellor to the lion. He could not bear to allow this happen. The jackal knew that what gives life to a man can also kill him. In his praise of the monkey's intellect, he was making insinuations of the lion's stupidity. His fellow praise singers being not as intelligent as him did not understand him. But the monkey being more intelligent than him understood the insinuations. The monkey got so intoxicated with their praises that he began to swagger in his walk. He began to say he thought the lion much more intelligent than he turned out to be. As they walked on, they came by a hungry crocodile lying by the riverside, his mouth wide open. It is only a fool that takes the yawning of a crocodile for a smile. Despite his intelligence, the monkey proved himself a fool when he took the yawning of the crocodile for a smile. Moving towards the hungry crocodile, the monkey drunk with praise said, "what an ugly-looking and I believe, stupid animal! Let me remove one of his teeth and hang it on my chest as a medal for my intelligence." The monkey stuck his hand into the mouth of the crocodile to remove one of his teeth and the crocodile snapped his teeth on the monkey's hand. The monkey provided the famished crocodile with his meal that day.

'I don't know who is blowing the flute of your own praise. But whoever he is, he is only taking you to an early grave. He is only feeding you to the crocodile. There is more to life than being intelligent. Two things make a man my boy: character and intellect. Character to me is much more important than intellect, for character can cause a damage no intellect can repair. So in your journey through the valley of life, your character sees you farther the path of prosperity than your intellect.

'Those who know should know there is something good in not knowing. Already those who do not know, know there is everything bad in not knowing, So I need not tell them the bad in not knowing. Those who may profit from my advice are those who know or think they know. Those who gain should know there is a loss in their gain and those who lose should know there is a gain in their loss. Life is always like that. There is always a little of good in what we see as bad and a little of bad in what we see as good.'

Chapter Seventeen

The Visit of the School Inspector

Every year the inspector of primary schools used to come to our school to inspect the condition of facilities and see if teachers were doing their job of teaching. Each year when he was coming, my headmaster would ask us to line up along the road he would be coming through to receive him. He used to come in a milk-coloured Peugeot 504 saloon.

Two days to his coming, my headmaster would tell us to wash our school uniforms so that they would look very neat when the inspector comes. Teachers were advised to make sure their lesson notes were in order and like the pupils, they were expected to turn out in clothes befitting their status. The latter advice if necessary was necessary only for Kantiok; for among our teachers he alone dressed shabbily. He had no more than four pairs of dresses and only one pair of shoes whose soles had worn out because of excessive use. Not only did Kantiok dress shabbily, he did not appear to be brushing his teeth as regularly as other teachers. His teeth always looked yellowish and his mouth often smelled. Sometimes traces of what he ate on a day were seen on his lips. Sometimes palm oil stains appeared on his shirt. The money Kantiok would have spared for dresses and to improve his general appearance, he spent on *burukutu*. He was popularly known as *kanuhuaa* – beer mouth. Most of what his mouth stank of was *burukutu*. As a pupil, when I looked at my headmaster, I found inspiration to become a teacher and a headmaster. But when I looked at Kantiok, I wondered if going to school and getting education could make a difference in one's life.

Though a drunk, Kantiok could teach well. That perhaps was his only redeeming quality. People said it was because he could teach well that my headmaster had not worked for his transfer or even sack. That could be. Another reason could be because teachers were not easy to come by, a teacher that undermined the high standing of the teaching profession like Kantiok instead of sustaining it, if he could not enhance it, was tolerated. Because of the scarcity of teachers, even primary school leavers who were good, were engaged as teachers to teach in the same primary schools they studied.

Unlike Kantiok, the other teachers dressed well and were always a spectacle to behold wherever they went in Sarai and the neighbouring villages.

The stones that lined the thoroughfare by the school frontage were always re-arranged in preparation for the coming of the inspector of primary schools. Sometimes they were painted white and green to further beautify the school. The flowers were given more water so that they would acquire a more lush appearance. Then my headmaster moved round the school more than he was wont to. One could feel in the air around the school that the school was expecting something grand.

Of all the visits of the primary school inspector, the one in my fifth year was more spectacular and memorable. That year my headmaster lined up the road the inspector would come through with large flags flying at full mast and gave little flags to us to hold and wave them at the inspector as he drove through our line-up on both sides of the road. It was a beautiful sight to behold. In addition, there was to be a march-past and a football match for the inspector. But the discipline prefect, Kantiok and the rain later spoiled everything for my headmaster and indeed for everyone. People even said Kantiok brought the rain because the rain started falling as soon as he turned up.

The inspector arrived the school about noon. We were all lined up along the road to welcome him. As he drove through our line-up in his milky Peugeot 504, we waved our little flags at him. Above our heads the wind was waving the big flags at him. He waved back at us and from the much of his face that I could see, he was very happy with the reception we were giving him. When he had passed through the guard of honour mounted for him by my headmaster, we all ran after his car as it made its way into the school arena where my headmaster was eagerly waiting. My headmaster had already instructed us on what to do after we had welcomed the inspector to the school on the road. Every pupil was to go to his class and sit down. So as soon as we entered the school, every pupil headed for his class.

The order of proceedings for the inspector's visit was that as soon as he arrived the school, he was to be taken round the classes to inspect their condition and in one class to sit down and listen to a teacher instructing the pupils. In another class, he would call on one of the pupils to tell him how he felt about his visit. After the class inspection, he would go to my headmaster's office where teachers would take their lesson notes to him, one after the other. After the lesson notes inspection, there would be a march-past and finally the football match.

My headmaster on receiving the inspector started taking him round the classes beginning with class one. The class inspection went very well until the inspector got to class six. It was at this point that things started going wrong. After inspecting the facilities in the class, he called on the discipline prefect to tell him how he felt about his visit.

This discipline prefect like others before him was all brawn, but no brains. He was discipline prefect on account of the strength of his arms than the fire in his head. He was a hunter in addition to being a farmer like everyone in Tyosa. He could chase a bush pig over twenty kilometres until he was able to kill it. One day he wondered to a friend how he could chase a bush pig over long distances and yet could not understand little, little things he was taught in school.

'Which little, little things do you mean?' the friend asked.

'*Mmm...mmm...kaih...*' he tried to tell the friend what he was finding difficult in school to understand, but could not.

'Is it A B C D?' the friend asked.

'Yes, yes,' he nodded his head quickly with a lot of relief on his face.

The moment the inspector called on the discipline prefect to speak, the face of my headmaster fell and everyone could see he was apprehensive he was about to be messed up.

'*Inpecto, sah,*' the discipline prefect began. *'I am very see to glad you, sah. Sah...'*

'Ok, ok. Enough, enough,' the inspector said, amused and sad at the same time.

My headmaster looked devastated.

'What manner of pupils do you graduate in this school?' the inspector asked my headmaster. 'A final year pupil speaking this kind of English?'

My headmaster looked apologetic. I am very sorry sir,' he said. 'But he is an exceptional case. The others are not like that.'

'How am I to know?' said the inspector. 'The only thing I know is that the only pupil in your school I asked to speak to me smeared your school with dirt with his very bad English.'

'I am very sorry sir,' said my headmaster, looking quite miserable. Pupils that were in the class said they had never seen him looking so sad.

After the class inspection, my headmaster and the inspector went to my headmaster's office where the school's teachers were to take their lesson notes to the inspector for inspection. The inspection of the teachers' lesson notes did not take time and soon my headmaster and the inspector were out of my headmaster's office for the pupils' march-past. The pupils were already lined up ready for the march-past. It was then Kantiok turned up with his shirt smeared with soup and his mouth reeking of *burukutu*. Three days to the visit of the inspector, Kantiok had sought my headmaster's leave to travel to his village to see his mother who he claimed was sick. He was expected to return to the school a day to the inspector's visit, but did not, until now.

It appeared my headmaster did not see him early enough. If he had, I am sure he would have found a way of going to bundle him out of the school arena so that the inspector would not see or know him as one of the school's teachers. It seemed he only saw him when he came close to where my headmaster, the inspector and other teachers were standing waiting for the march-past to commence. As soon as my headmaster saw him, he became livid with rage. In a way, he had been happy that Kantiok was absent during the inspector's visit and had asked another teacher to stand in for him in his class. Now he had turned up to smear the school with a bad name after smearing himself with *burukutu* and palm oil soup.

'Welcome sir,' Kantiok said in a drunken voice, extending his hand to the inspector for a handshake.

'Who is this fellow?' the inspector asked, scoffing the offered hand.

Before my headmaster could say anything, Kantiok said, 'I am one of the teachers of this school.'

'Is that true?' the inspector turned on my poor headmaster in disbelief.

'Yes,' my headmaster murmured.

'Terrible!' exclaimed the inspector. 'No wonder you graduate pupils with such bad grammar.'

The inspector scarcely closed his mouth when rain started pouring. Everyone scampered to his class. The inspector scampered into his car and was driven off from the school. Kantiok stood under the rain gaping at my headmaster, stupidly.

Chapter Eighteen

Tyrant of the Football Field

A day after the visit of the primary school inspector I had a fight with the school football captain. I never liked sports, football in particular. The only games I had something close to a liking were volleyball and pole vault. Both these games, however, were not developed in our school and excited little interest among the majority of the pupils. The main sports for boys were football and athletics and for girls basketball. In the school, if a pupil could not play football, he was less regarded by those who could and even those who could not, no matter his other talents.

The football captain was also the athletics prefect. I suspected the reason for this was that football and athletics in the school were seen as one thing and took place in quick succession. All physical exercises took place during the long break. First, pupils run round the football field, mostly three times. After this, they would all go into the field and be parcelled into small groups for different physical exercises. Each group was headed by one prefect or the other. Often each group formed a circle to play. Usually when the circle was being formed, the prefect in charge of the group would be saying, 'form a circle,' and the pupils in his exercise group would say, 'a big circle.' After forming the circle, the pupils might do press-down, hop up and down or hold each others' hands and run round, throwing their legs sideways. If the prefect desired the pupils to do an exercise like frog-jump which entails dismantling the circle, he would dismantle it and carry out that exercise. But at the end of the various exercises in the football field, the pupils in a group without the supervision of a prefect would most likely form another circle holding each others' hands and running round kicking out at one of their number who was outside the circle and who was required to catch any pupil in the circle sluggish enough to be caught. The one caught would become the new outcast to be kicked at. As the pupils in the circle ran round aiming their legs at the outcast outside the circle, they would be shouting, '*Bastard, bastard-bastard! Kick out at him, bastard!* Of course, if my headmaster heard this song, the skins of the pupils that sang it would certainly be angry with their mouths that day. A game of football followed immediately after the various physical exercises in the football field.

During the athletics session round the football field, all the school pupils would run ahead of the football captain and athletics prefect who would run behind flogging those too lazy to run fast. I believed that in his mind he would be singing, '*Bastard, bastard-bastard!*' as he lashed out at those who could not run fast enough. I was always among those who could not run fast. So the captain's whip was always very close to my skin. Like the discipline prefect during my primary one, he did not like me. Like the discipline prefect the reason for his disliking me was that I was brilliant in class and he was not, though unlike the discipline prefect, he could speak good English. While I respected him for the brilliance of his legs, he was not ready to respect me for the brilliance of my head. So he was always on the look out for me during athletics to deal with me if I lagged behind during the running round of the football field.

Even with the eyes of my headmaster everywhere, I loathed running so much that I often dodged the school's athletics session by staying away from the football field during athletics. Initially, the football captain did not understand my tactics, but eventually did. When he did not see me during athletics having earlier seen me in the school this day, he came for me after his football game.

'Nto, why didn't you come to run like other pupils in the football field today?' he asked.

'I am not well,' I lied

'Why are you not well?'

'I don't know.'

'Why did you come to school if you are not well?'

'Learning in class, is it the same thing as running?' I asked, getting angry.

'Don't be insolent,' he said, pointing his finger threateningly at me.'

'I am not insolent,' I said.

'Even if you are not well, are you aware you need my permission to stay off the track?'

'I am not aware,' I feigned ignorance of what I knew very well.

'I can see you are beginning to assume more airs than is good for you. Kneel down,' he commanded me.

'I will not,' I said.

He slapped me and I slapped him back though I knew he was my senior and much stronger than me. Before I knew what was happening I was on the ground with the football captain on top. He was hitting me on all parts of my body. I caught hold of his hand and bit him with all the power in me. He cried and jumped off me as other pupils rushed in to separate us. We were both taken to my headmaster by the head boy who among all the prefects appeared to me the most humane.

'What is the matter?' my headmaster asked in a hard, grating voice. It was a damp, windless morning that seemed to have eaten up any humour he might have in him. He did not appear to be in the mood to be involved in pupils' squabbles.

'They were fighting sir,' said the head boy.

'Fighting?' my headmaster asked, getting interested. Of all the rules he had made for the school, that against fighting appeared to be the one he reserved his most severe attitude for.

'Yes, they were fighting,' said the head boy.

'Now that is a very serious matter,' said my headmaster. 'Nto why were you fighting?' he asked me.

'He first attacked me, sir,' I said.

'Why did you attack him?' my headmaster asked the football captain.

'Sir, he is a lazy boy,' said the football captain, nursing his hand where I had bitten him. 'He will not run round the football field like other pupils.'

Is that true,' my headmaster asked me.

'Yes, it is true sir,' I said. I will never lie to my headmaster.

'This is what I like about you, Nto – never telling a lie,' my headmaster said, his hard face dissolving into a soft, pleasant mien. He was looking at me admiringly.

'But he lied to me,' said the captain. 'He said he was not well that was why he did not run.'

'Is that true?' asked my headmaster.

I was now in a quandary. My headmaster saw me as a symbol of truth. If I admit I lied to the captain, he would be terribly let down and that would change his opinion of me. If I deny the claim of the captain that I lied to him, I would be lying to my headmaster though unknown to him. The latter appeared the best option for me. 'I did not tell him I am not well, sir,' I said, managing to keep a straight face.

The captain could only look at me dumbfounded. My headmaster's eyes were also on me and from the expression on his face I could see he believed me. He had so much come to expect the truth from me that he would not associate me with a lie. I was very happy.

'Captain, you should not have attacked him if he was not at the race track,' said my headmaster. 'You should have reported him to the head boy or to me.'

'But, today is not the only day he dodged sport.'

'The more reason you should have reported him much earlier. You are to blame Captain,' said my headmaster.

'But sir…'

'You have no defence, Captain. When you don't discourage a wrong doing by taking steps to nip it in the bud, it gains confidence and begins to assert itself as right.'

As my headmaster spoke, from the corner of my eye, I could see Ngai the old man whose mangoes we plundered four days ago entering the school. My heart lurched. How could my misdeeds be rising up against me all at once?

Chapter Nineteen

Yashim, What is Your Name?

Ngai was an old man with a blind wife and a son of about four years. His house was at the outskirts of our village, on the path to school. He had about three mango trees in front of his house which returning from school hungry we always went to pluck. He had tied a bad medicine on a stick and hung it on all his mango trees in the most visible way to scare us away from his mango trees, but we were only scared for a while. When we lost our fear of his medicine, even with the eyes of my headmaster on us, we used to descend on the mangoes like a pack of hungry vultures, which in a way we were.

The most potent medicine Ngai would have hung on his mango trees that would have scared every child and adult away from his mango trees were the leaves of the *nensham* tree. *Nensham* was the tree of the ancestors. No one used it for firewood. Only the ancestors used it to kindle their fires. The leaves of the tree were seen only in the *Aboi* shrine and in any farm or fruit tree where they were used as bad medicine to scare thieves away. Women and children in particular had about as much fear for *nensham* leaves as they had for *akrusak*. No child or woman dared move near a farm or fruit tree on which *nensham* was hung. But Ngai could not hang *nensham* leaves on his mango trees because the leaves of *nensham* were the symbol of the pagan religion of *Aboi-abyin* and Ngai was a Christian.

A certain pastor had preached to Ngai to repent of his sins now that he was old and nearer the grave so that when he dies, he would go to heaven instead of hellfire. Ngai had repented though he did not know what he was repenting of, though he rarely went to church and though he still drank *burukutu*. The songs of the church when he went to church did not move him as the songs of *Aboi-abyin* during the *Aboi* festival. Whenever he heard the cry of *Aboi-abyin,* he always had a new sense of well-being. He had boundless joy whenever *akrusak* danced past him. He would fix his eyes on the dancing steps of the fearsome mystique with a deep smile that showed happiness and fulfilment. One Sunday while in church, the congregation stood up to sing a song under the guidance of the service leader. Midway into the song, Ngai forgot he was in church and started singing the song of *Aboi-abyin* and even taking the dancing steps of the dance of the ancestors. The person standing close to him nudged him and he was sort of startled to know he was in church. A baleful look replaced the radiant countenance hitherto on his face.

Yet Ngai was a Christian who could not hang *nensham* leaves on his mango trees. To do so meant he had left Christianity and surrendered his soul to the devil. Old and with a blind wife, Ngai was helpless against our onslaught with the collapse of his wall of defence – his medicine.

Ngai had the apotropaic gift of speaking to death to be reasonable. Before his conversion to Christianity, three young men in Tyosa had died in quick succession. People said they were *eaten* by witchcraft. A meeting was called at Afang-zuk where serious issues affecting Tyosa were always discussed. Ngai spoke at that meeting with the authority of years and wisdom. 'The eyes of the people of Tyosa do not want to see this kind of evil again,' he said. 'The ears of the people of Tyosa do not want to hear this kind of evil again. If anyone in Tyosa has a hand in this evil, the mouth of the people with which I speak, places a curse on that person.'

While speaking, he did not face one direction. He would face the east and speak to the eastern wind thrusting his walking stick forward and stabbing the ground with it now and then. Then he would turn and face the west and speak to the western wind. After he had spoken, he struck the earth with his walking stick. Dust rose into the air like smoke from a smouldering fire. He raised his stick from the ground; the impression of the stick on the ground was very visible for everyone to see. If the people at the meeting had spoken with one mind, the following day when they returned to the meeting ground, the impression of the stick on the ground would still be there even if there was wind or rain before they returned. When the people returned the following day, the stick impression was not there. It meant the people had not spoken with one voice. Another meeting was called in which Ngai and other elders spoke like they did in the previous meeting. Evil people were warned to give up their treachery or face unpleasant consequences. At the end of this meeting, Ngai again struck the earth with his walking stick. The following day when the people returned, the stick impression was still there. The people had now spoken with one mind. Since that day, no young man died again in Tyosa.

To return to my fear over Ngai's surprise visit to our school, four days ago, we made the old man to cry when he could not stop us from plucking his mangoes. We were about eleven returning from school. As usual, when we came to Ngai's mangoes, we stopped to pluck some to eat on our way home. Ngai was at home and appeared more determined that day to prevent us from plucking the mangoes. The moment he heard our movements inside the mango trees, he came out of his house with his walking stick to chase us away.

We quickly divided ourselves into three groups. When he chased one group away, the other two groups would swoop down on the mangoes. When he left the group he was chasing to chase another group, the group he had abandoned would move in on the mangoes. At a point he was so desperate to hit one of us that he picked up an unripe mango lying on the ground and threw it at a boy a mango tree was between him and. The mango hit the tree and bounced off to hit Ngai on his right leg. In frustration he started crying. Though some of us started laughing at him, I felt very sad and immediately left the place and proceeded home.

Now Ngai was at our school. What could have brought the old man to the school? I wondered, fearfully. Had he come to report us to our headmaster for discipline?

When my headmaster received a complaint against a pupil by someone who was not part of the school community, he would call a special assembly to address the complaint before the complainant. That was what he did when he received Ngai's complaint. He wanted everyone in the school to hear from his mouth the punishment he would hand down to those the old man had reported so that those who might be tempted to tread their path would be deterred.

At the assembly, my headmaster called out the names of those the old man had reported. I was surprised there was no name of any of us that made the old man to cry the other day. I had jumped to the conclusion it was that incident the old man reported, not knowing it was another incident that took place the previous day. These boys were reported not for plucking the old man's mangoes, but for stealing his pawpaw which he appeared to cherish more than the mangoes. The pawpaw tree was behind the old man's house while the mango trees were in front. I never knew he had a pawpaw tree until he lodged his complaint.

When all the pupils my headmaster had called had gone to the front of the assembly, he started calling them one after the other again. First, he called Yashim and said, 'Yashim what is your name?'

Yashim answered, 'my name is Yashim.'

'Look at this old man and tell me if he is old enough to be your grandfather.'

Ngai was sitting on the edge of the veranda my headmaster was standing. The old man was sitting with his walking stick on the ground and his two hands placed on the head of the stick to provide a resting platform for his chin.

Yashim looked at Ngai and said he was old enough to be his grandfather.

'Will you steal from your grandfather?'

'No, sir.'

'Why then did you steal from this old man?'

'I am sorry sir,'

'The question calls for an explanation, not apology.'

Yashim did not say anything.

'Well, my boy,' said my headmaster. 'Your conduct calls for restitution and this is my order of restitution for the old man. From today, you shall go to work on his farm for an hour every day till the end of this rainy season.'

I looked at the old man and I could see him beaming with satisfaction.

Next,' my headmaster beckoned to the next boy who he condemned to fetching the old man's drinking water and washing his clothes until the end of the rainy season. The boy called after this one was to fetch firewood for the old man.

After handing down his punishments, my headmaster turned to Ngai and said, 'Baba you did well reporting them to me. If you abandon your clothes in anger to a conscienceless person, he would wear them to tatters without a thought.'

The old man left the school that day a very happy man. When he was coming down from the veranda where he sat while my headmaster was handing down his draconian sentences, he was laughing. His mouth being without teeth, it was a laughter that had no shine in it. The sun that would have given glory to his laughter had long set. Being without teeth that would hold his saliva in his mouth, his saliva was drooling out of his mouth as he laughed. He flicked his walking stick stylishly in front of him and walked away from us with a swagger.

My headmaster's punishments were very strange. But there was no appeal. His judgment was like God's judgment. One could only pray my headmaster did not pass any judgment on him. If he did, there was no remedy.

Before the old man brought his case to my headmaster, my headmaster had never given these kinds of punishment. The punishments left those on whom they were passed lame with shock and the rest of the pupils petrified. After my headmaster's verdicts, no pupil was seen again near Ngai's pawpaw or indeed his mango trees. However, older people went to steal from the old man.

Chapter Twenty

A Recipe for Anomie

We had always thought we were the only ones who stole Ngai's fruits. It was when we stopped stealing from him we found that older men were also stealing from him. A week after Ngai left our school, the pupil who was sentenced by my headmaster to fetch water for Ngai was returning from the river with a bucket of water when he saw a man using a bamboo stick to pluck pawpaw from the old man's pawpaw tree. Neither Ngai nor his wife was at home.

He immediately changed the direction of his movement so as not to be seen by the man. After he had quietly brought down the bucket of water he was carrying, he tiptoed to a vantage position where he could have a better view of the man. It was Baushe. The pupil was surprised that Baushe an elder in the church could steal and steal from an old man like Ngai. Immediately he knew he must report the matter to my headmaster. He was already serving a sentence for stealing the old man's pawpaw. If he did not report what he had seen, he would be accused of further stealing from the old man, an accusation he was sure would earn him a more severe sentence than the one he was now serving. But if he goes to report to my headmaster, Baushe would be gone with the pawpaw by the time he returns. Then he would deny stealing the pawpaw. If he could steal, he would think nothing of denying he stole. His best option was to confront the thief now and report his stealing later.

He greeted Baushe.

Baushe nearly jumped out of his skin in shock and fright. The bamboo stick fell from his hand. He turned and saw the pupil standing behind him.

'I have caught an old tortoise that will not follow the paths like other animals,' said the pupil,' very pleased with himself.

'Eeeh, it is not what you think,' Baushe stammered. I was trying to pluck this pawpaw for Ngai. You know these old men. They can't do anything for themselves.'

'Well, I don't know about that,' said the pupil, looking at him with disbelief. 'Why didn't you help him fetch his water?'

'But you are already doing that for him.'

'Why didn't you cut the grasses around this house? As you can see, there are so much grasses around the house. Why didn't you cut the grasses that can bring snakes into his house instead of plucking pawpaw for him?'

'Well, you know how it is.'

'I don't know how it is. How is it?'

'Trying to help people can sometime land you in trouble.'

'You are a thief. You are not trying to help anyone.'

Baushe could only clear his throat.

'And you are an elder in the church.' Seeing that Baushe was at his mercy, the pupil acquired more audacity than he ordinarily had. 'How does it feel to steal and tell lies as an elder in the church? You must feel like the old tortoise our headmaster told us about.'

'Please, let this be between me and you,' Baushe pleaded. 'You can have the pawpaw I plucked. You don't need to give it to the old man. He won't know. You know he is almost blind like his wife.'

'Was that why you came to steal from him?'

'I beg you take the pawpaw and say nothing of this happening to anybody.'

The pupil collected the pawpaw from Baushe and his face brightened up.

'This is not your pawpaw,' said the pupil.

Baushe's face fell.

'Why should you bribe me with what is not yours? Why don't you give me that your big cock? You know your offence is a grievous one.'

'Please accept the pawpaw and forgive me.'

'Where is your heart?' asked the pupil.

Again Baushe cleared his throat.

'Well, I won't do what you recommend. Why should I? If I have such a mind, I would have plucked the pawpaw myself. Why should I wait to receive stolen property? I have the opportunity to steal the pawpaw myself.'

'You are beginning to sound like a pastor to me,' said Baushe, looking at the pupil in a sly manner. 'But you don't deceive me. You are not that decent and honest. I know you once stole the same pawpaw from the old man and he reported you to your headmaster. You are now fetching water for the old man to serve the sentence your headmaster passed on you.'

You are right there; that is why I am going to report you to the pastor of your church so that he also passes his own sentence on you. Maybe he will recommend you take over the water fetching from me or fetch firewood for the old man. I will also report you to my headmaster in addition to reporting you to your pastor.'

'I am not your headmaster's pupil.'

'Your children are in his school.'

'Please don't report me to your headmaster, for the sake of my children.'

'You should have thought of them before coming to steal from an old man.'

'I beg you in the name of God.'

'In the name of God, you shouldn't have stolen; especially from an old, helpless man.'

From where they stood, they could hear the sound of an approaching motorcycle. My headmaster was coming. Baushe's face was now a tablet of misery while the pupil was skipping about with joy. Baushe darted off, but the pupil expecting such a move held onto his dress. He was much stronger than Baushe and he began to drag him to the path my headmaster would ride through.

Soon the country meadow and foliage surrendered my headmaster to their view.

When my headmaster got to where the pupil and Baushe were, he stopped his motorcycle and inquired what the matter was.

'Sir, he had stolen from the old man,' said the pupil, breathlessly. 'The pawpaw I stole and you condemned me to fetching water for the old man, he had stolen. And he is an elder in the church.'

Although Baushe was an acquaintance of my headmaster, on issues of this nature, my headmaster had neither friend nor acquaintance. Now he was behaving towards Baushe as if he had never known him. 'What this boy said, is it true?' he asked Baushe, rolling out his big eyeballs at him.

Baushe did not say anything, but guilt was all over his face.

My headmaster knew that Baushe was an elder in the church, but he still asked him, 'Is it true that you are an elder in the church?'

Baushe nodded.

'That makes things easy,' said my headmaster. 'The pastor must take care of his own as I am taking care of mine. Call me the pastor,' he said to the pupil.

The pastor's house was not far away. The pupil still enjoying the temerity that Baushe's theft had invested him and forgetting my headmaster was with him hollered, 'pastor!' from where he was standing.

'Are you mad?' asked my headmaster, looking quite grave.

The pupil was immediately brought to his senses. He ran to the pastor's house and soon he and the pastor were seen coming together.

Not many people in Tyosa knew where the pastor came from. Some people said he was from Watyap while others that he was from Makwaku. He was a quiet man, but a veteran preacher. He worked tirelessly to convert the ancestral worshippers of Tyosa to Christianity. Every Sunday he preached of hell fire and the need for

Christ's followers to forsake all heathen practices to avoid going to hell after their death.

'Pastor, you have not been holding your flock well,' my headmaster charged as soon as the pastor and the pupil came to him.

'What is the matter headmaster?' asked the pastor, dumbfounded.

'Your elder has stolen Ngai's pawpaw,' said my headmaster.

'Is that so?' the pastor asked Baushe, looking very alarmed.

'Sorry pastor,' said Baushe, looking woebegone. 'It is the work of the devil.'

'The convenient defence again,' hissed my headmaster. 'I think Christianity has a lot to thank the devil for. The faith won't survive without him,' he remarked with a heavy dose of cynicism. 'I think you ought to be sending some of your tithes to the devil for him to continue to keep quiet in the face of your frequent false accusations.'

'Headmaster, that is not a proper thing to say,' said the pastor, heatedly

'So I should sympathise with him for being the victim of the devil's treachery? Where does that leave the poor, old man whose pawpaw has been stolen?'

'In whatever situation we find ourselves, we should be wary of sinning against God with our tongues,' said the pastor.

If the pastor had hoped to create remorse in my headmaster, there was nothing on the face of my headmaster to suggest he had succeeded in doing so.

'Every scoundrel puts his sins on the devil,' said my headmaster. 'The devil must be stronger than Jesus Christ to carry all the sins of the world without crying out in pain. Pastor, the devil must be very patient. Patience is a godly attribute. So the devil might be said to be godly in certain respects.'

'Terrible,' muttered the pastor in revulsion of what my headmaster said. 'I did not know you have wandered this far from the faith. Still, I maintain you are not saying the right things,' the pastor protested.

'I love and revere Christ, if you don't know,' said my headmaster. 'But his church has disappointed me. Talking about right, is it right for a Christian to steal; an elder in the church for that matter?' my headmaster charged, all the veins in his neck bulging to a rupturing point. 'You can't hold your flock properly and you are talking of proper and improper things. I don't believe in buck-passing. I believe in responsibility. Hold your flock and you will have less need of the devil.'

'We are trying.'

'How many times have you stolen from the poor old man?' my headmaster asked Baushe, ignoring the pastor. 'This can't be the first time. A thief is never caught the first time.'

'This is the first time,' Baushe murmured

'So it is only today the devil visited you?'

Neither Baushe nor the pastor said anything.

'Were you eating rats as a child?' my headmaster asked Baushe.

'Why are you asking such a strange question?' asked the pastor.

'It is not so strange,' said my headmaster. 'You know rats steal a lot. People who ate rats as children are wont to steal.'

The pastor laughed in spite of himself.

'Pastor, will you say you have been fair to Ngai?' my headmaster asked, turning on the pastor dramatically.

The pastor's face became grim. 'What do you mean by that question?' he asked, somewhat bewildered.

'Have you been fair to him by converting him to Christianity?'

'Only the devil can doubt the benefit I conferred on him by converting him,' said the pastor with a look that hung between severity and amusement.

'Pastor I am the devil in that case and I am happy to carry all the sins of the world, at least the sins of Christians who blame me for all their human failings.'

'Why, headmaster should you ask such a question?' asked the pastor.

'I asked such a question because by converting the old man, you have laid him bare. If he were not a Christian, no one dared touch his pawpaw or mangoes because *nensham* leaves would be hanging on them. Now you have made him a Christian and he cannot hang the leaves of the ancestors on his fruit trees. You made him abandoned *Aboi-abyin,* then unleashed thieves and bedbugs on him. That to me is ungodly. Pastor, you know what? You are not better than Achan the son of Zimri. You have stolen from Ngai what is most vital to him: his security and sense of self-worth. You deserve to be hanged. You killed his soul the day you promised him a soul in heaven and got him converted to your faith. Now when he dies and gets to heaven, he would find he has no soul to enjoy the eternal life you said awaits him in heaven wherever heaven is. What you did to the old man wouldn't have been too bad if you can restrain your flock. But you can't restrain your flock and they are straying into people's farms. If an elder of the church can steal, what do we expect of ordinary members? Now, Ngai has lost both his trap and the bird the trap was meant to catch. After your people have stolen his pawpaw, you will still expect him to pay tithes and during harvest, you will expect him to bring the fruits of his trees. This is what sounds ungodly to me.'

'This is more than what I can bear,' the pastor murmured in agony. 'I can't stand this any longer,' he said, beginning to walk away.

'Restrain your flock pastor!' my headmaster shouted after him. 'Take care of your charge and I will take care of mine. Do your duty. I am doing mine. In fact, it is because I have done my duty that your elder was caught. I will do more for the old man.

Tomorrow you will see *nensham* leaves hanging on every fruit tree in this house. Hell; where is it?'

Like my headmaster promised, to the shock of everyone *nensham* leaves were seen hanging on every mango and pawpaw tree in Ngai's house the following day. Even Christians had a morbid fear of the leaves of the ancestors because they knew of the ugly and painful boils that afflict anyone sacrilegious enough to steal anything on which *nensham* was hung. From that day, no one was ever caught stealing from the old man again. But it was difficult to say whether it was because of the *nensham* leaves or because Baushe was caught stealing Ngai's pawpaw.

Chapter Twenty-One

The Underbelly of An Angel

Very few pupils knew that my headmaster and Kantiok attended the same college and that while in college they were friends. Why their past relationship was unknown to many was that neither my headmaster nor Kantiok spoke about it. While my headmaster would not want to be associated with a drunk like Kantiok and so would not talk about their past as friends in college, Kantiok though a drunk who should have no shame was in his sober moments ashamed of the fact that his classmate in college was his headmaster and so would not talk about their college life. But when he was drunk and free from shame, Kantiok used to talk about their college life with my headmaster, telling anyone that cared to listen about their friendship and the kind of rascal my headmaster was in college. The problem was that not many people believed a drunk and so not many people believed my headmaster and Kantiok were in the same college and that they were friends. Curiously, however quite a number of people believed Kantiok's stories about the rascal past of my headmaster.

A little over a year after the inspector's visit, Kantiok was in a *burukutu* house drinking the fermented liquor with all the excitement and satisfaction of an alcoholic. He and four of his friends were sitting around an old *assuum* – a pot of *burukutu*, they had bought from the *burukutu* seller. They were sitting in front of the house where the liquor was sold. Each man had in front of him a big calabash into which his share of the liquor when fetched from the liquor pot was poured. Inside the liquor pot was a small calabash that was used to distribute the drink. By tradition, sharing of the liquor was done by the youngest member of the group and Kantiok was the oldest. But Kantiok thinking he would not get his fair share if someone else did the sharing always manoeuvred himself to the position of being the one to share. Being the one sharing today as always, he was seated closer to the pot.

'Kanuhuaa, don't you think it is a bit too early to start drinking?' said one of the drunks. His calabash was already filled with *burukutu* and he was taking it to his mouth as he spoke.

'Who said we are drinking?' asked Kantiok with a mischievous gleam on his face. 'My friend, we are only having early morning devotion.'

All the drunks roared with laughter.

'If you have a long journey,' said one of the drunks, 'it is good to start early. It is always a long journey before any of us here gets drunk. So it is only wise that we start the journey to our destination early.'

As they drank the liquor, they talked of all matters under the sun. Kantiok looking at the sky said he did not like what he was seeing there. 'The rain that is falling this year is the urine of the honey bear, not his tears. The urine of the honey bear is as poisonous as the urine of a rat,' he said with a sagely bearing that a drunk could put up.

'Kanuhuaa, you don't mean it,' one of his fellows said, looking at him admirably.

'I mean it,' Kantiok said.

'That means there will be little harvest this year.'

'You can feel it in the air,' Kantiok said, waving his left hand in the air. 'But don't worry. There will be enough for *burukutu* to still be brewed. But there may not be enough to pay tithes with. But that is the headache of the pastor. Let him bear his pains as I am bearing mine.'

'Kanuhuaa, you are a sinner.'

'I hear you,' Kantiok belched.

'Kanuhuaa, when the devil is in town, he stays in your house.'

'That is when he misses his way to your house and he has never done so.'

'Kantiok, you should repent of your sins.'

'I agree; but I can't see any pastor I will repent before. The pastors have left the pulpit and entered the world to look for mammon. Christ saw it coming before we all saw it. Money is the root of all evil. It is threatening to remove God from the hearts of all men and plant the devil there. I tell you money is the first and last enemy of God. Beer is only a demon. Money is the devil. In fact beer in the long run may be found to be God's best friend. A drunken man envies no one. As a matter of fact, I have been thinking of issuing a posthumous award to whoever invented beer. His invention has brought more happiness to the world than any invention of man you can think of.'

'Kanuhuaa! You may have a bad mind, but your head is still sitting on your neck,' said one of the drunks.

'The devil these days seeks to embarrass God even in the church. You can still remember how Bobai entered the Church two years ago on Christmas Eve with the calabash he had drank *burukutu* with on his head,' said another drunk.

'Even proper caps are not allowed to enter the church on the head of anybody,' said Kantiok, taking his calabash full of *burukutu* to his mouth.

'Yet Bobai entered the church with a calabash of *burukutu* on his head as his cap. When he was being sought to be walked out of the church by the usher, he protested that he also had come to worship God. Imagine!' said the drunk seated to the left of Kantiok

'You can also remember what Tabat did in the church,' said another drunk. 'After the pastor finished delivering what some people called *a-life-changing sermon* and called for repentance, Tabat who was a drunk, a womanizer and a chain smoker stood up with three of his friends and walked to the pastor on the pulpit to repent of their sins. As they walked towards the pulpit, the fellow bringing up the rear whispered to the fellow walking in front of him that he should remind Tabat they were not going to a beer parlour, but to the pulpit to repent of their sins before the pastor, lest he forgets and light a cigarette. Perhaps the message was not relayed to Tabat. As soon as the pastor finished praying for them, Tabat reached for his cigarette right inside the church.'

Some of the drunks laughed at this.

'What you said reminds me of a joke I heard recently,' said the drunk sitting behind Kantiok. 'Someone said he was in the church one Sunday and was so shocked to see his friend lighting a cigarette that he spilled the beer he was drinking.'

All the drunks laughed at this joke.

'You may not know why this religion of Yahweh forbids drinking alcohol,' said Kantiok. 'I will tell you. This religion would rather live with court jesters and pretenders than someone who tells it the home truth. A drunk does not pretend. He says it with his mouth as it is in his mind.'

'You know something Kanuhua, I think you have said something there,' said one of the drunks. 'It is not that the religion of Yahweh, or the one they called Islam resent alcohol or have contempt for it. I suspect these religions fear alcohol. These religions fear the honesty of alcohol because there is something not altogether straight in them which alcohol will expose.'

'Everyone you see in this world is a liar and a pretender,' Kantiok said, shaking his head violently as if to settle a raging war going on there. 'They are all cowards. It is only we they call drunks that are honest and bold enough to tell life what it needs to hear for its own good. As an honest man, when I die and get to heaven I pray God will give me a plot of land to erect a beer parlour there. Heaven I tell you will be hell without beer. Even here that there is beer, you know how things get bad on any day there is no beer.'

'Kanuhuaa!'

'What I see coming is very bad.'

'Since when did you become a seer?'

'I am a great medicine man in my village, if you don't know.'

'Whoever takes your medicine will die of liver cirrhosis.'

'Well, you know death itself is some form of healing. There is no healing that will make you not to need medicine again like death.'

While other people always placed their calabash on the ground after drinking, Kantiok held his calabash in his hands, nursing it affectionately. He took long pulls at the beer wiping his mouth with the back of his hand each time he took off the calabash from his lips. Occasionally he belched to express satisfaction and give indication that he had created more room in his stomach for the liquor. He was on the fourth calabash when my headmaster rode past them on his motorcycle.

'The hell with him,' Kantiok spat, spilling some of the *burukutu* in the calabash in his hand on the ground. 'I say the hell with him!'

'Why are you swearing at the headmaster,' one of his friends asked.

'Damn him,' Kantiok hissed. 'Who is he?'

'He is a headmaster and you are a common classroom teacher,' said another man.

'Who wants to be a headmaster? Let me tell you something. This calabash of *burukutu* in my hand is worth much more to me than a headmaster.'

'I am glad you said to you.'

'But, come Kantiok, what is your problem with Bamai?' asked another drunk.

'You mean you don't know? And you call yourself my friend? This *burukutu* must have over flooded your memory. How many times will I tell you I and the big ass were in teachers college together? He was an average student while I was always topping the class. But look at him today and look at me. He is a headmaster and I am not even an assistant headmaster; is that fair?'

'Is that a question to us or the calabash in your hand?'

'You are an idiot. Imagine; the asshole is now a headmaster.'

'But you just said who wants to be a headmaster,' one of his fellows reminded him.

'It wasn't he that spoke that time. You know this thing we drink has its own voice. The hand could be that of Esau, the voice may be that of Jacob,' said another fellow.

'Yes, who wants to be a headmaster?' Kantiok belched again. 'Forget what I just said. You know in college things were great. Even things that were bad were great. There was no pump or well in our school. So we fetched the water for our meals from the river. It was compulsory for each student to go to the river to fetch the water for our meals. But you wouldn't believe the cheap lie these asshole who calls himself a headmaster told the head boy of the school to escape fetching water with us.'

'What lie did he tell him?' his fellows asked him when he paused and appeared not keen on continuing his tale. But it was a bait to arouse their interest and get more attention than he was getting.

'He said he had an operation on his head and so could not carry heavy things. But you don't know the sad thing.'

'What was the sad thing?'

'The stupid head boy had no brains to ask the asshole to show him his head and so he got away with a lie that wore a red cap with an eagle feather on it. We ground our sculls while the asshole lay in bed laughing at us.'

'But this shows he was smarter than you.'

'Perhaps so. But the fellow could take big risks and get away with them. Even now I still don't know how he got away with some of the risks he took. I think he must be the favoured child of the devil. You know there are certain fortunes the devil puts aside for his children. Bamai no doubt is the devil's child and it appears the devil has been taking care of his own. Water was like gold in our school. The crook after lying to be exempted from fetching water had the audacity of bathing with the water of his house captain when it was taken to their hostel's bathroom by the junior student who had brought it from the river to the hostel for the house captain to bathe. As soon as the junior student placed the water in the bathroom, Bamai ran into the bathroom and used the water to bathe. When the house captain went into the bathroom to bathe, it was the empty bucket he found. Do you know who suffered for it? It was the innocent junior student. The house captain never believed he brought the water in the first place because it was unthinkable that any student could have the nerves to bathe with water fetched for the house captain. Not many students in our school even suspected Bamai's capacity for mischief.'

'I tell you the guy is smart,' said the drunk sitting to the right of Kantiok. Of all the drunks, he spoke less.

'No, not smart, but street wise,' said Kantiok. 'You know there are people like that: dull in class but clever on the street. The asshole had always been that sort of fellow. We were five in our group, just like the five of us sitting here. We were all living in one unused toilet and bathroom attached to one of our classes. We constituted ourselves into some form of union. We had a president who was the leader of the group, a secretary who keeps the record of our activities, an informer who informed us that the bell had gone off for us to go to the dining hall, a rusher who bulldozed his way into the dining hall on a day students rushed to cart away food in the dining hall and a storekeeper who kept our excess food and other valuables. This asshole said I should be the secretary because I was more brilliant than all of them. He also nominated Buta who looked like an *ako* tree to be the rusher. Do you know who he recommended for storekeeper?

'Himself!' a drunk shouted.

'You bet,' said Kantiok. 'That is how cunning he has always been. He has a way of always manoeuvrering himself into a soft spot. Even this headmaster office he now occupies, there must be a way he manoeuvred himself into it.'

'So rusher did the donkey walk while Bamai presided over the loot?'

'That was it,' said Kantiok, with what sounded like a note of bitterness. 'On any day there was a rush on the dining hall, we were sure that was the day we would have more food in our room. Buta would shove everybody aside and grab so much. He would then run off with what he had grabbed. No one dared follow him. There was a day he carried a whole sack of bread and ran off with it to our room without anyone chasing him to retrieve some of the bread. All the students were scared of him because of his size and brute strength. After he had deposited his loot in our room, if he felt he had not grab enough, he would run back to the dining hall and grab more. When we have eaten what we could, what was left was handed over to the asshole as storekeeper to keep in a big locker in our room. The key to the locker was in the care of your man as the storekeeper. He opened it only when he wanted to. Not even the so-called president could make him open it. Not even Buta who sweated to bulk it in could ask him to open it. To this very moment, I don't know why we put up with his arrogance. But that was how it was.

'Buta, what a name!'

Yes that was his name and it was not a nickname. It was the name his father gave him and it fitted him like a glove,' said Kantiok. 'Oh, I nearly forgot to tell you a black day in the career of Buta as a rusher. There was this night that there was a rush in the dining hall. Buta grabbed four aluminium dishes full of food and as he was trying to make away with them through a window of the dining hall, somebody slapped him across his face and he dropped the dishes on the ground. Before he could recover from the shock of the attack, the fellow who slapped him carried the dishes and ran off with them into the darkness.'

For a while, the group including Kantiok who told the story, reeled with laughter. There is something inexplicable about group laughter. When a person says a funny thing or recounts a funny tale to himself, he may not laugh. But when he tells the same joke or tale to another person or a group of people, he would laugh when the others are laughing.

When the laughter subsided, the drunk who spoke less said, 'so Bamai was such a smart fellow at school?' Though he spoke less, he seemed to be the one stoking the flames of discussion whenever they were flagging.

'To me that is not smartness,' Kantiok said. 'If you say he was a trickster and a mischief, I will shake your hand. One day our school principal came to assembly holding one of the aluminium dishes used to serve us food. Everyone was surprised to see the principal holding an aluminium dish with flies buzzing over it. The principal tilted the dish so that we could see what was inside. Behold the dish was half-full with shit. There was no curse the principal did not place on whoever defecated inside the dish and left it behind one of the classes. I suspected Bamai as the culprit; but since I did not see him do it, there was nothing I could do.'

'Wonderful!' exclaimed a drunk.

'That was not all. In fact Bamai once persuaded us to kill someone's goat that strayed into our school and we did. Buta chased the goat and caught it. But when it was slaughtered and fried, Bamai as storekeeper kept the fried meat.'

'What a guy! Kanuhuaa, I tell you that is my man.'

'There is more to admire your man for,' said Kantiok belching loudly. The smell of the *burukutu* coming from his mouth seemed to have acquired a more virulent stench than the one coming from the *burukutu* in the calabash he was holding. Even his fellow drunks, who ought to be immune from the odour, winced at the stink coming out of his mouth.

Kanuhuaa, the *burukutu* in your stomach had been rejected, probably because it is too poisonous for your intestines,' said one of his fellows. 'Now you are feeding the air with it. This could make the air drunk and that is dangerous.'

'I can see the air carrying the *burukutu* he has vomited into it towards the pastor's house,' said the drunk sitting to the right of Kantiok.

'God forbid bad thing,' said another drunk, snapping his fingers, shaking his head violently and hunching his shoulders.

'Like I was saying,' continued Kantiok, moving the calabash towards his mouth. Whenever he belched, he had a sense of having lost some of the *burukutu* to the air and therefore he must refill immediately. It was like he had just gone to the toilet and needed to eat something to replace that which was lost to the latrine. 'Bamai as a senior student seeking to punish some junior students for no offence at all gave them toilet paper to wash and iron before him. The toilet paper should not in anyway be damaged. When they could not, he beat them. He was known among junior students as World Wicked. But his wickedness was not only for the junior students. Even his seniors were not immuned from his wickedness. You know in the boarding school, students sleep on double-decker beds. The senior student sleeps on the lower bunk while the junior sleeps on the upper. Whenever the junior is to climb up to his bed, he would put his left foot under the mattress of the senior and heave himself up onto his bed. Never is he to place his foot on the mattress and bedsheet of the senior. But Bamai as a junior student did not always exercise the care a junior should when climbing the double decker bed to sleep. Often, he would put his foot on the mattress and bedsheet of the senior and hurl himself onto his bed. His senior was a very patient student and used to overlook what Bamai was doing. But Bamai encouraged by impunity began to assume more airs and graces. One day he came with his feet covered with mud and stepped on the white bedsheet of his senior and heaved himself onto his bed. His senior could not take this and punished him by asking him to wash all the toilets of their hostel. Bamai submitted himself to the punishment, his impenitent heart seething with vengeance. A month after serving his punishment, Bamai unseen by anyone pulled out his bed from its hinges and left it literally hanging on the bed's fork. At night when his senior was in his bed to sleep, Bamai climbed onto his bed and he and the bed came crashing on top of his senior below. That was how wicked and bad that fellow could be.'

'Did he get away with this one also?'

'The sad and shocking thing was that he did. The devil like I said look after his own.'

'It is then not a bad idea to have the devil as a friend,' said the fellow seated in front of Kantiok.

'You can say that again,' said Kantiok. 'But even the devil if he must not be surpassed in evil by some of his disciples does occasionally allow them to be reproved by punishment. And that was what he did when Bamai had the effrontery of calling one of our female teachers out of the class as if she were his girlfriend. 'Our school had no uniform. So everyone wore what he liked to class. One day the trickster turned up in suit when all of us were already in class taking an English lesson from a female Philippino teacher. Instead of entering the class, Bamai stayed outside with his back to the class and sent a junior student to go in and call the Philippino teacher. The philippino teacher seeing only his back and thinking it was a staff from the state ministry of education rushed out of the class only to find out it was your man who burst into laughter. The poor woman did not return to the class, but headed for the principal's office to lodge a complaint. The good thing was that Bamai did not get away with this. When we came out of class for break, we saw him felling a tree the principal said he must not only fell, but uproot the stump after felling the tree.'

'Ahh....' One of the drinking fellows snorted.

'You pity him?' asked Kantiok. 'Well, it wasn't bad all the way for your rascal. My eccentric principal made him a prefect in our form five.'

'Made him a prefect? That is interesting.'

'Don't you think Bamai manoeuvred his way to become a prefect over you?'

'No. he couldn't have manoeuvred his way into this one.'

'But how could your principal appoint a scoundrel like him a prefect?'

'My principal if you don't know was an eccentric character. In fact, looking at him later in life, there were many things he and Bamai had in common.'

'Even for an eccentric man, I still say it was strange to make Bamai a prefect.'

'Imagine, Bamai was made a school prefect over you.'

'Kanuhuaa, so you have always been his subject.'

'It was not over me he was prefect, but over his fellow deviants.'

'That guy had always had it the way he wanted.'

'This one wasn't a good one,' Kantiok butted in. 'Our school was a boarding school. So going home for weekend was prohibited. But your headmaster and other rascal students like him would always find a way of getting out of the school and going home for weekend. From intelligence reports coming to our principal, Bamai was the most notorious student leaving school and going for weekend. So our principal appointed him *a-weekend-going prevention-prefect.* It was his responsibility to stop all those leaving the school and going for weekend from doing so. It was bizarre, but our principal was a bizarre character. From that day, Bamai never left the school and went for weekend again. You know, the rat does not eat the fish kept in its custody. When a thief becomes so notorious, he is given the key to the store to keep. From that day no student could sneak out of the school and go home for weekend because Bamai knew all the paths they used and stalked them like the demon he was. But when Bamai and his fellow rascals were no longer going for weekends, the school which used to know quiet during weekends because of their absence became noisy. To me, the school was better off during weekends without these rascals than with them. Without them we read our books more. But with the rascals prevented from sneaking out, their mischief which they would have taken outside was turned upon the school.'

The response to this tale was not as animated as the earlier tales by Kantiok. The longer they stayed in the *burukutu* house, the less they had to drink and the more sober they became.

'Each of us carries his rotten egg in his mouth,' said one of the drunks. 'It is he who breaks his own in public that people turn up their noses at. The headmaster is a wise man. He has not broken his rotten egg before any of us. Instead he had carried it into the bush and buried it there. But you Kantiok are a foolish man. You took your rotten egg to the market and broke it. That is why everyone is turning up his nose at you.'

'Do you know something Kanuhuaa,' said the drunk sitting in front of Kantiok. 'Shame is a strong emotion with those who are ambitious and I think you are ambitious. In your sober moments, you are ashamed to tell people how you and Bamai who is now your headmaster were at school.'

'That is very true,' said the drunk to the left of Kantiok. 'Fear and shame are twins you will always find in those who are ambitious. Usually fear is for failure. Therefore when failure comes, fear disappears. Kanuhuaa has already failed and so fear has left him. Where fear used to sit in his heart, shame now sits. Shame comes to mourn failure and you can even hear its lamentation in Kanuhuaa now. He is a man that is beyond fear.'

'That is where I will always disagree with you,' said the drunk sitting behind Kantiok. 'For all you don't know, some of us might be drinking this *burukutu* out of fear.'

'You are talking rubbish; total rubbish,' someone hissed.

Just when they had nothing more to drink, somebody walked past them and entered the *burukutu* house. Kantiok did not show any sign that he had seen him. But as soon as the man bought the liquor and sent it to them outside, Kantiok asked if he heard his greeting when he was entering the house.

'It is time we call it a day in this beer house,' one of the drunks said, shifting uneasily on his seat. 'We still have many houses to go to and I will like to return home early. You know I work with the

Local government council at Kachia. I wouldn't want to be late to work tomorrow. My boss is a queer fellow who insist on punctuality to office.

'You have not said anything,' said Kantiok.

'Kanuhuaa, I agree with Shingkut that we should always retire home early,' said one of the drunks. 'You are small and slight of frame. If you are sacked from your job, you may walk past without anyone seeing you and pointing a gossiping finger at you. What of Shingkut? He is so big that he can't avoid notice.'

Chapter Twenty-Two

Jokes and our Little Skulls

When my headmaster rode his motorcycle past Kantiok and his fellows drinking *burukutu* in the beer house, he came by an old lorry carrying wood and hurtling to Zonkwa. Almost every day this lorry was driven empty past our school to more remote villages and came back loaded with more wood than it was meant to carry. The lorry driver waved at my headmaster, but as was customary with him, he did not wave back.

A few days after my headmaster rode his motorcycle past the old lorry, the lorry again was driven past our school full of firewood. To ensure the old lorry carried more firewood than its size allowed, after it was stacked with firewood to the brim, some of the firewood it was carrying were stuck up at the edge of the lorry's trunk and more firewood were stacked against what might be called an extension of the trunk of the old lorry. Three hefty men were sitting on top of the wood. They looked hungry and bad tempered.

Because of its age and the weight of the wood it was carrying, the trunk of the lorry was swaying from side to side according to which side the uneven muddy road tilted it. It was a very frightening spectacle to behold. As it drew level with the school we started chanting:

Rain, thunder come and fall
Three huge men are on a lorry
Come and pound some big fat men.

This was always the song we chanted whenever the lorry went past our school. My headmaster had warned us to desist from the practice, but the urge in us to sing the song whenever the old lorry was moving past our school was too great. My headmaster on his part did not seem to be serious in his warning. In fact, some pupils said he enjoyed the song because a faint smile used to lurk beneath his stern visage whenever we were singing the song. Young as we were, he must have seen our chanting as the harmless pranks of little children. But the men on the old lorry did not see the matter that way, at least that day.

Usually when we chanted this song, those in the lorry would just look away without saying anything. But today as soon as we started chanting what had become our greeting to the old lorry, the tree men sitting on top of the lorry started throwing the wood the lorry was carrying at us. Everyone was shocked. Pupils started running helter-skelter to avoid being hit by the pieces of wood coming from the old lorry. Within a short time, the assembly had scattered. My headmaster stood on the veranda watching in shock and visible anger as pupils ran away to avoid being hit by the flying pieces of wood. As suddenly as the attack started, it stopped.

My headmaster and all our teachers came out of the veranda into the open field where the assembly was only moments ago. In place of the assembly were pieces of wood littering the assembly ground. For sometime, my headmaster stood in one spot surveying the scene in disbelief and anger. He looked towards the road, but the old lorry was gone. He began pacing about picking the pieces of wood one by one and dropping them back on the ground again. But the last one he picked up he did not drop on the ground, but flung it at the road the old lorry had passed through.

From our classes, we stood watching my headmaster and our teachers on the assembly ground. When my headmaster was tired of pacing about, he began walking towards his house across the road. Soon we heard his motorcycle roaring. Everyone knew what he was going to do. He was going to give the old lorry a chase.

My headmaster did not return to the school till towards closing time. Immediately he returned, he called an assembly. Everyone knew something was coming.

For sometime, he stood looking at us his eyes smouldering with anger. 'Do not think I sympathise with you over what happened this morning,' he began. 'Rather I am angry with you and myself. I allowed my lambs to wander far away from home and I must thank God the hyena only howled at them. I left my chicks to go beyond the winnow where my eyes were on them and I can hardly blame the hawk swooping down on them. When a father allows his child to laugh too much today, he is only preparing him for tears tomorrow. A wise father would rather his child cry today so that he can laugh tomorrow. I did not behave like a wise father when I used to see you laughing at the men on the lorry and did not flog you. What was the result? This morning we were all crying.

'It is only those who climbed the tree with their teeth that know how bitter the tree is. I have climbed the tree of life with my teeth and I know how bitter it is. I should have told you who think it is a sweet tree how bitter a tree it is. I have seen the world more than you and I ought to tell you it has more tears than laughter in it. The world, if you don't know, is a synonym of misery. That is why an Atyap man would say a child is being done the world when the child is being maltreated. You may see medicine and think it is couscous. But I should know better. The shame of the medicine man is unimaginable when the corpse of his own child is being carried away for burial. How would he now be seen by those who thought he had medicine for all ailments? That is my shame now. When I was a child, a one-eyed man came to our house. Both my father and mother were in their rooms. When my mother heard the man's voice from her room, she asked who it was and I with the innocence of childhood said it was a one-eyed man. Though as a child I was innocent, I was severely beaten after the man left. In fact, I would have been beaten in his presence if that wouldn't have served to increase his embarrassment. The same thing happened when a stranger to our house was given food by my mother. The man was a fast eater. Not long after he was served the food, he thanked my mother for the meal. My mother thinking he had not eaten much of the food said, "you did not eat the food?" It is a remark our people are fond of. It is a courtesy paid to a stranger. I was sent to carry the leftover of his food. When I opened the calabash and saw that the stranger had eaten all the food, I called out to my mother that the stranger had eaten all the food. Both my mother and the stranger were embarrassed. But I could not be beaten in the presence of the stranger as that would serve to further embarrass him. So my mother had to wait until he left the house. It was then I received the beating of my life and warned never to say such things in the presence of strangers. I was innocent, no doubt. But innocence is not enough. From that day, I began to understand the ways of the world and to follow them without coming to harm.

'Like my mother taught me that innocence is not enough, I should have taught you that innocence is not enough and steer you away from harm's way. But I did not. That is why I called this assembly to chastise myself, then chastise you. From today on, never and never you pray for evil for someone in the presence of who you wish ill for. Anyone who does that will soon cry more with the same mouth he laughed. You can go.'

We all left the assembly for our classes without my headmaster telling us what happened when he chased the old lorry. It was the following day I found out what happened from the lorry driver.

Chapter Twenty-Three

The Trip to Zonkwa

The following day was a Saturday. It was Zonkwa market day. After close of school on Friday, my headmaster called me to his office before I left for home. In his office he told me he had nine bags of guinea corn he would like to be conveyed in the old lorry to Zonkwa market the following day. He said I should accompany the guinea corn to the market as he would not be in the lorry. Rather he would follow us behind on his motorcycle.

That night I did not sleep. I had never rode on any automobile before and the thought of riding on one the following day gave me such happiness that I found difficult to contain. When I left the headmaster's office after receiving the good news, I started singing and sang all the way home. Everyone in my house was surprised to see me so happy.

'Nto, why are you so happy?' my father asked me.

'Tomorrow, our headmaster is sending me to Zonkwa with his grains on a lorry!' I said and waited for the exclamation of happiness I expected to follow my declaration. But instead of the excited response I expected from my father what I got was a cold query. From the faces of some of my siblings who had just returned from school, all I saw was scorn and envy. Like me, none of them had ever ridden on an automobile. Why should I be the first? But from the face of Anthony one of my siblings, all I saw was joy and good will for me.

'Which lorry?' my father asked, 'Certainly not the one that wanted to kill all the school children this morning?'

In my happiness, I had forgotten our unpleasant experience with the old lorry in the morning. My siblings who reached home earlier no doubt had already informed my father about it.

'It is the same lorry,' I said with most of my excitement gone.

'You will not follow that lorry,' my father said with an uncommon note of finality.

I looked at the faces of some of my siblings and all I could see now was happiness.

'But, daddy, it is the headmaster that has asked me to accompany his guinea corn to Zonkwa market in the lorry,' I protested.

My protest had the effect I thought it would. It was unthinkable for my headmaster to send a pupil on an errand and his parents to prevent him from running the errand. It was much easier for my headmaster to postpone the parent's errand by asking the pupil to run his first. My father in his shock over what the lorry men did that morning which had just been reported to him had forgotten how revered my headmaster was. From his facial expression after my protest, it was clear my protest had brought back that reverence.

'I forgot it is your headmaster's grains you will be taking to the market,' he said in a voice one might say sounded penitent. 'Of course, you will go and I know no harm will befall you. They dare not touch a child that is on the headmaster's errand.'

'But the headmaster was there when these men threw logs of wood at us this morning,' Sankwai who appeared to envy my being on the lorry the following day more than my other siblings said, desperately, looking downcast.

Even without this new fortune that was coming to me, Sankwai seemed to have always envied me. Although he was three years my senior in the primary school, he had repeated three times and we were now in the same class. Though we were now in class six, he could still not write a letter. So I wrote his letters for him. Usually, he would call me to a hidden place with a paper and pen in his hand and beg me to write a letter for him which I often did without asking for anything in return. But one day, when he beat me, I told him that henceforth he had to be writing his letters by himself. Knowing the implication of the threat, he begged me to forgive him.

'This is different,' my father said. 'You were not on the headmaster's errand when they hurled woods at you. And did they just hurl woods at you? Didn't you invoke rain to come down and beat them? If you send a dog after me, if I have a hyena I will send it after you. If Nto does not taunt them while in their lorry, why should they harm him?'

After my father had spoken, all my siblings except Anthony left the house. Anthony was much closer to me and he never seemed to envy me like my other siblings. He stayed with me when the others left and I told him once more what my headmaster told me in his office and my expectations of how delightful it would be to ride on the old lorry. In his nature, he was very happy for me and wished he could go with me.

'You cannot go with me,' I said to him, touched by his attitude. 'But whatever I get from the trip, I will share it equally with you.'

He was happy with what I said and we went on to talk about other things, often returning to my trip to Zonkwa on the old lorry the following day.

At night sleep was long in coming and short in staying. I kept turning on my bed eager for morning to come. When I heard the first cockcrow, my heart rose in happiness. I was getting closer to riding on the back of an old lorry, for it never occurred to me that as a boy sent by my headmaster, I would be asked to sit in front of the lorry with the driver.

Early in the morning, I went to a little stream near our house and took my bath. Anthony accompanied me to the stream. He asked me to buy him *panke* when I get to Zonkwa and I renewed my promise to him the previous day. I believed my headmaster would give me some money after he sold his guinea corn.

Usually the stream was cold in the morning, but I did not feel the coldness this morning. Quickly I finished taking my bath, and Anthony and I went back home where I put on the clothes my mother bought for me for the last Christmas and headed for Sarai. As I was leaving, I could hear Sankwai chanting:

Rain, thunder come and fall
Three huge men are on a lorry
Come and pound some big fat men.

Like me, he supposed I would ride on the back of the old lorry and was wishing me a rain bashing. My heart quaked at the song. It was then I knew the agony we had been subjecting the men on the old lorry.

At Sarai, I was surprised to find the old lorry already parked in front of my headmaster's house. I prayed it had just arrived because I would be unhappy to have kept my headmaster and the lorry waiting. I was relieved when I moved near the lorry and saw my headmaster's guinea corn being loaded on it. It meant it just arrived.

It was a different headmaster I met in his house. His hair which was always well combed looked unkempt and his body was covered with dust. The trousers he wore were torn at the knees and the shirt he wore looked like it had been brought out of a pot. It was so ruffled that one would think it had been stitched into folds. Generally, my headmaster looked like he slept in a cave and was just emerging from the cave he slept in with the clothes he slept in.

Two of the three men that threw logs of wood at us the previous day were in the lorry arranging things. One of them looked like an ape that was aspiring to be a gentleman while the other looked like a reformed drunk. The driver was on the ground tying what looked like yam in an old fertilizer sack.

I greeted my headmaster and he smiled genially at me. I had never seen him smiled that way and I was strongly moved. All the dirt and unseemliness that characterised him were removed by that smile. I smiled back at him.

'You are welcome Nto,' he said, going about his tasks in the house. 'You may sit down on that bench,' he said, indicating a bench that stood near the wall of his house. I sat on the bench and reclined my back against the wall. My headmaster disappeared into one of his rooms. Soon his wife came out with a loaf of bread and tea for me. All pupils in the primary school called her Madam. In my primary one, I thought that was her name. It was much later I got to know her name was Abigail. She was such a humble and quiet woman that her presence was hardly noticed. When she gave me the tea, she went back into the room and I never saw her again up to the time I left the house in the old lorry.

I received the bread and tea from my headmaster's wife, my hands shaking slightly. Though I had eaten bread, I had never drunk tea before. In fact I had never seen it, though I had heard about it. I thought the tea would be as hot as my mother's porridge, but it turned out a lot hotter. As I raised it towards my mouth, the steam coming from it warned me tea was not to be drunk the same way I drank my mother's porridge. The first contact between my lips and the tea in the cup told me tea was a liquid flame of fire. Instead of sipping the tea, I was nibbling at it like a rat that was not sure of where it was. Although I was making little progress with the tea in my left hand, I was making much progress with the bread in my right hand. When my headmaster observed the way I was drinking the tea, he advised me to be dipping the bread in the tea. I started doing so and taking tea became a pleasure for me, not an ordeal. By the time I finished taking the tea, the lorry was ready to move. My headmaster told me to climb into the lorry and that he would soon follow us behind with his motorcycle. I nodded my head and made to climb into the back of the lorry, but the driver told me to go and seat in front. I looked at my headmaster and he nodded his head.

The driver led me to the front of the lorry and helped me onto the front seat. The man who looked like the reformed drunk also got into the front seat to sit beside me. The ape climbed the back of the lorry to sit among the sacks of corn and other goods carried by the old lorry. But for his colour, there were more ways he looked like a sack himself than a human being. The driver went round to seat on the driver's seat. He started the old lorry and it came to life on the instant. He pressed the throttle and a booming noise filled the air. He engaged gear and the lorry began to move. I waved at my headmaster and he waved back at me.

Shortly after we took off, the driver told me to relax and feel at home. The lorry was as much the headmaster's as it was his. He told me my headmaster had apologised to them for our unruly behaviour of the previous day when he gave them a chase and caught up with them. So the headmaster's pupils were their children.

I was very happy to hear this and it removed any fear I had about the driver and his men in the lorry.

The road was very bad and progress on it by the lorry was very slow. I could now see how easy it would be for my headmaster to catch up with us on his motorcycle. While the old lorry had to cover the whole road and so could not avoid big potholes on the road, a motorcycle could easily do so by picking only the good part of the road. So my headmaster could go back to sleep and still be able to catch up with the lorry before it got to Zonkwa.

Sometimes the lorry had to literally come to a halt to be able to move past very bad portions of the road. Whenever this happened, I involuntarily looked into the back of the lorry to see if the ape and the sacks of corn were still there. I did not trust the ape. He could push the sacks down and drop off without our hearing anything, given the deafening noise of the old lorry. The lorry kept inching forward like a millipede that had lost one of its antennas. A distance of fourteen kilometres was going to take us almost one and half hours.

About 9.30 am we came to the worst part of the road not far away from Zonkwa. It was muddy, marshy and slippery. The tyres of the old lorry were worn out and so had no bite on the road. When we got to this part of the road, the driver adjusted his sitting position. He was now sitting on the edge of his seat gripping the steering very tight. The road here had widened into a small football field because drivers in trying to avoid the bad portion of the road often left the road and drove in the bush. In a muddy road, if the first driver did this successfully, he left behind impressions that other drivers followed to avoid the bad road. Soon the new road became as muddy and slippery as the old road and there would be need for another road until it was impossible to create another road again.

Because of the wideness of the road here, the driver was undecided which part of the road he was to take. First, he made to take the left side, but thinking the middle was better, he attempted swerving to the middle. The worn out tyres of the old lorry slipped and sank into the mud. He eased the pressure of his left foot on the clutch and pressed the throttle harder to pull the lorry out of the mud. But this only helped to settle the tyres deeper into the mud. When the lorry would not move despite his pressure on the throttle, we all came down and I was shocked to see that one of the rare tyres was almost completely buried in mud. In my mind, it would be impossible to bring out this tyre from the mud and move the lorry beyond this point. Even the driver did not seem to be sure he and his men alone could pull out the lorry from the mud. For sometime, the driver and his men did not know what to do. If the lorry was to be pushed, the driver would have to be on the driver's seat to control the steering. That meant he would not be part of the pushing. That left the two men and I .It was clear that the two men and I could not push the lorry out of the mud. Yet, in desperation, we attempted doing so, but only succeeded in besmirching ourselves with mud and driving the tyres of the lorry deeper into the mud.

There was now fear and panic in the eyes of the driver and his man who looked like a reformed drunk. It was only the ape that appeared unruffled by what was happening. He advised that we get the leaves of trees and tree branches to wedge the lorry while we are pushed it to prevent it from sliding back. We all spread out into the bush to get the leaves and small tree branches. We were still in the bush when I heard the sound of my headmaster's motorcycle. I was sad and happy at the same time. I was happy because my headmaster might help us get out the old lorry from the mud. I was sad that we were yet to deliver his guinea corn to the market. From what my mother told me, those who got their commodities early to market got good prices for them. Those who brought them late often had to accept any price or bear the additional cost of taking them back home when the market closed.

When my headmaster saw us, his motorcycle began to lose sound and speed until it came to a halt a few metres from the lorry. He came down from the motorcycle and exclaimed, 'what I feared has happened!' But despite his exclamation, he looked calm. He sympathised with us over what had happened and joined us in getting leaves and tree branches to help bring out the lorry from the mud. Though we started gathering the leaves and branches before my headmaster, there was little difference between what he gathered and what any of us gathered when it was decided we had gathered enough and we should begin to take the leaves and branches to the lorry.

When we had wedged the rear tyres with the leaves and tree branches my headmaster assigned roles to each of us. The driver, the ape and I were to push the lorry. The reformed drunk was to push in the wedge as soon as the rear tyres lifted a bit. My headmaster was to drive the lorry. Until that day I never knew he could drive a lorry; and it seemed the lorry driver too. But the ape knew my headmaster could drive, for he told the driver that my headmaster was a good hand on the wheel when the latter asked my headmaster if he knew how to drive.

'There is nothing on four wheels that I cannot handle,' said my headmaster as he climbed into the driving seat.

He started the engine and at the count of three by my headmaster, he engaged gear and we pushed. The rear tyres lifted and the reformed drunk pushed in the leaves and tree branches. But by the time the tyres settled back on the wedge, he was all covered with mud. I believed it was because of this unpleasant aspect of his assignment that my headmaster did not assign that responsibility to me. Otherwise being the less strong among them, the reformed drunk who was stronger would have been more useful pushing the lorry than wedging it. On the third push, the reformed drunk did not even have to push in the leaves and branches because the tyres of the old lorry did not slide back again. The lorry was out of the muddy and slippery road and set to totter on again.

My headmaster came out of the lorry and waved the driver on. We all climbed in and the lorry began to move again. Already we could see the rooftops of Zonkwa.

Our graduation party was only ten days away. My headmaster used to refer to our graduation party as the last supper. If I was able to make something out of this trip, I would buy a shirt, a pair of trousers and shoes that I would wear for the party. As the Master of Ceremonies at the party, I would receive maximum attention if I could afford to dress well. But whatever I did with what I got from my headmaster, I knew I must fulfil my promise to Anthony.

Chapter Twenty-Four

The Last Supper

My headmaster and our teachers used to attend the graduation party of the final year pupils of our primary school merely to give the graduating pupils homilies and leave. They did not eat the meals prepared by the pupils for their party. It was demeaning for a teacher to eat food or even drink water before his pupil.

It was during the homilies that my headmaster used to tell the graduating pupils that what they were about having was their *last supper* with him though they would not have it with their master physically present. That he would not be there physically for them to have their *last supper* with him did not mean he was not with them in spirit.

Every pupil knew what my headmaster was saying was true. Though he was never with the pupils during their eating and drinking, reverence of him was never far away from them. After the homilies, my headmaster and the teachers would go and leave the pupils to start their party.

In those days, parties by final year primary school pupils were common and popular. For my class, preparation for our final year party started in our year five. To get money for the party, we went to work on farms of people who had money and wanted to hire labourers. By the time we were in primary six, we had about four hundred naira. For some of us, this money was more than what we needed for the party. But some of us, particularly the big boys and old men in the class felt it was not enough. According to them, we needed about five hundred naira to have a *last supper* that had never been seen in Sarai primary school.

It was difficult to tell my headmaster's attitude to final year parties. He neither seemed to like them nor discourage them. If his attitude to these parties must be classified, it would be classified as indifferent or ambivalent. Though he might be said to be indifferent, he always had an eye on what was going on at the party venue.

A few days to our party, my headmaster suddenly took ill. It was surprising to everyone because he had always been a healthy man full of life. No one knew what the cause of his sickness was. But it looked quite serious on the first day. He was taken to the missionary hospital at Zonkwa. At the hospital the cause of his sickness could not be diagnosed. He was returned home without medication because the doctors said they could not prescribe any drug for a sickness they did not know.

Back in Sarai there were rumours that my headmaster had been attacked by spirits of the mountain. That was why his sickness could not be diagnosed. Everyone knew that my headmaster liked hunting and hunted mostly alone. A day before he fell sick, he had gone to the forest to hunt antelopes and guinea fowls. According to rumours he had pursued an antelope into a cave in a mountain where he saw a dog and an old woman sitting inside the cave. He had abandoned the chase and ran back home only to fall sick the following day.

My headmaster who could have confirmed or denied these rumours could not speak. Even if he could speak, not many people would tell such a tale to my headmaster and ask him to confirm or deny it.

The following day, my headmaster recovered as miraculously as he had fallen sick. Every pupil in our school was happy that he was now well and would attend our party to give us a homily. Since he fell sick, an uneasy quiet had pervaded the school. The school was like a river and he was the water that gave it life and the authority of a school. Now that he had recovered and returned to the school, water had returned to the river and there was life in it once more.

Preparations and talks about our *last supper,* which had lain prostrate during his sickness, began to rise and flourish again.

We wanted to buy a cow, but the outrageous sum the Fulani man was demanding for his emaciated cow could buy us four healthy goats leaving even a balance to cover other expenses. In the end, it was the goats that were purchased. The pupil that was the chairman of the party committee at first appeared to be a very frugal person. He wanted every kobo given to his committee accounted for. But members of his committee and indeed the whole class soon discovered that his frugality did not extend to money to be allocated for beer.

Beer as one of the refreshments to be purchased for the party was a hotly debated issue because before our time, no other graduating class had ever bought beer for its party. But our class had more money than previous graduating classes, and as it turned out, had more drunks. There were many pupils in our class who were not our age mates. They were fully grown up married men who wanting to become literate had enrolled at the primary school. Most of these fully grown adults were drunks and by their sizes induced fear in the younger pupils. Though less intelligent in class, they compelled obedience and regard outside the class on account of their strength. In an argument with the younger pupils, they had a way of winning the argument, sometimes not by the superiority of their reasons, but by the force of their veiled and sometimes naked threats.

On the matter of whether beer should be purchased for our party or not, most of the younger pupils had argued against it; but the old men supported by a few younger pupils who themselves were drunks, argued that beer must be purchased. One of the old men said he did not take soft drinks and since soft drinks were to be purchased to meet the taste of pupils who took them, beer must be purchased to meet the taste of those who took it. What was more, everyone knew he and his fellow drunks being bigger and stronger, always farmed more than we the little ones when we were working for the money to be used for the party. That being the case, they had more right to determine what was to be done with the money than those who contributed less to earning it. From the way he spoke, anyone listening to him could see that he was not putting a plea forward, but a demand founded on right. The last point he made, which none of us could hardly dispute, gave his right a wild authority among us. So it was agreed that beer would be purchased. But the older pupils quickly warned us never to allow my headmaster hear of the matter. For, if he did, he would not allow it. According to them, the previous graduating final year pupils had also wanted to buy beer, but my headmaster had stood against it. He had told them that one could not use a viper to tie firewood and expect to get home well.

When we were forming the party committee, we did not know the drunks had met secretly among themselves and resolved to have many of their members in the committee to protect and advance their interest. In fact the idea of a party committee was mooted by one of them. Before our class, there had been no such committee. The whole class had planned its *last supper*. But when the idea was mooted in our class, it appeared sound. So it was accepted. Drunks in line with their secret pact nominated their members into the committee and when the committee sat to choose a chairman, a drunk nominated a fellow drunk. In the end, we were saddled with a committee of drunks to organise a sacrament my headmaster called our *last supper*. The party organised by drunks, what we had at the end of the day was not a *last supper*, but a carouse.

The chairman of the party committee while sparing expenses for other party victuals spared no expense for alcohol. It appeared to non-beer drinking members of the committee that whenever the chairman was trying to reduce money allocated for a given item, he was doing so to add to the money to be used to purchase beer. He showed a particular grudge for the money allocated for soft drinks. In his mind, he must have thought it was wasted money.

On the day of the party, cooking of food and frying of meat started early in the afternoon in the school area. The cooking and frying were done by the girls. But the boys were never far away from where the girls were tending the pots. They kept coming and going as the cooking and frying progressed.

By 7.30 the evening of the party, we were all seated at the party hall. My headmaster and our teachers were there with us. After two teachers spoke some words of advice to us, my headmaster began his homily:

'In anticipation of music, the young antelope was almost dancing itself lame. What will it do now that the music is about to start?' my headmaster began.

Quite a number of us shifted uneasily on our seats. So my headmaster despite his sickness had not missed the excitement on our faces as we prepared for the party.

'Yes,' continued my headmaster, looking intently at us. 'Now you are about to leave this school and go into the world. If in normal times, the bat engages in extreme acrobatic dancing, what will it do when it is crowned the dancing queen of the air? Even under my watchful eyes, some of you have been rascal in their conduct, what would they do when they leave this school? Whatever you do, know that it is the firewood you gather in your youth that you will sleep with at night during your old age. Whoever sows the wind in his youth will surely reap a whirlwind in his old age – a time he can hardly bear any wind of whatever kind.

'Those of you with character and intellect will do well. Those without character and intellect may not even qualify to be the servants of those with character and intellect. You might have sat in the same class and played together during break-time; but I tell you some of you will have to say *sir* to their classmates in the years to come. Know this that whenever you hear anyone saying *sir* to you, you were the one that first said *sir* to yourself and he is merely echoing your voice. Likewise, when people look at you with contempt, it is you who first looked at yourself with contempt and the world is merely throwing back at you your due. In this world, no one, except perhaps fortune, gives you anything you have not given yourself. You might have been of bad character in this school, but there is time to make amends and start on a clean slate outside the school. There was no sinner like Saul, but there was no apostle like Paul.

'Whatever you would eat and drink in this hall this night would be the last thing you would eat under my care. I might not be here in body to eat and drink with you, but you know as always I will be with you in spirit. This is my last meal with you and that is why I call it our *last supper*. Eat and drink in memory of me.'

My headmaster's speech was so touching that some pupils were moved to tears by the time he finished. Immediately he was through with his homily, he and the teachers filed out of the party hall leaving us to start our party.

The party started by 8.30pm. There was a doorman at the entrance of the classroom where the party was taking place. He was a fully grown adult and one of the drunks of our class. He was so big and strong that no one could dare him. That was why he was made a doorman to ensure no one who was not an invitee to the party entered the party hall. There was a light-man who was in charge of light. There was no electricity in Sarai and no one owned an electric generator that we could hire. So we had to use a blowlamp. The light-man was a very tall man who could without standing on a bench or a desk hang the blowlamp on a nail driven into one of the beams of the roof. I who was the Master of Ceremonies was by common consensus the most eloquent speaker of English in our class and that was what earned me that office, though I was also largely seen as a shy person. My fluency in English apart, the unbending vernacular rule of my headmaster operated to make my class favour me with the office of Master of Ceremonies. If we appointed someone less fluent in English and he spoke vernacular in the course of performing his duty as Master of Ceremonies, my headmaster despite the fact that we were graduating pupils will fine the entire class if he happened to know of this.

The party started on a fine note and progressed on a fine note until it was time for dark dance. As its name implies, dark dance was a dance in darkness. The light of the blowlamp was put out and for about thirty minutes, boys and girls particularly the matured ones would be fondling each other in the dark. Before the light was put out, boys, for it was unthinkable a girl would be so wayward as to approach a boy, would have placed themselves 'within striking distance' of the girls they fancied. As soon as the light went out, they reached for their heartthrobs and began to fondle them. The dark dance in our party took place after those taking beer had drank their beer. Even some of us who were not drunks needed, in addition to the darkness, the courage that beer gives to touch the girls they liked. So they too took beer.

But in our party there was one boy that had a different plan for our dark-dance. When other boys were moving closer to girls when the light was about to be put out, he was moving closer to the doorman who had always terrorised him. In his pocket was a needle he intended to use on the doorman as soon as the light was out.

Shortly after the light was put out, we heard the doorman who was already drunk screaming in pain that the light-man should put on the light. This boy who happened to be my closest friend in our class, but who never told me what he planned to do was at work jabbing the doorman with his needle. The light man not knowing what danger we were all in quickly lit the blowlamp, but the boy had since run away from the doorman and was lost in our midst. The doorman was swearing that if ever he laid his hand on the person that jabbed him with the needle, his dress would tear to shreds when he slaps him. It never occurred to us to conduct a search on our bodies for the needle so as to fish out the culprit, and so my friend got way with his misfeasance. It was the following morning he told me he was the one that was jabbing the doorman with the needle and even showed me the needle. Having gotten away with mischief, he regretted that instead of a needle, he should have brought a fishing hook with a line on it which he would hold at a distance and be pulling the hook which he had already buried in the flesh of the doorman, to inflict maximum pain.

To return to the party, after the light-man had brought back the light, the doorman did not allow the light to be put out again. The party continued with eating, drinking and dancing. Towards dawn, there was commotion at the door where the doorman was on guard. Someone wanted to enter the party venue by force, but the doorman would not allow him. I and a few pupils went to the door to see who it was only to find to our shock that it was Kantiok.

It was unheard of for a teacher to return to a pupils' party after the headmaster and the teachers had had their last words with the pupils before the start of the party and left. But Kantiok was always the sort of person things which had not been heard of before were heard of from him. He returned drunk to our party spilling obscenities everywhere. The doorman too was drunk and did not care a hood whether or not Kantiok was his teacher. He was calling him a *blodiful,* about the only word of English he could pronounce near accuracy. We all pleaded with him to allow Kantiok into the party hall, but he would hear none of it. He could not even bear any of it. Before we knew what was happening, he had broken the beer bottle in his hand and was threatening Kantiok with it. Kantiok on seeing the broken bottle started screaming. It was his screams that woke my headmaster and brought him to the party venue.

When my headmaster saw Kantiok screaming and the drunken doorman holding a broken bottle in his hand and advancing on Kantiok, he passed out. He was rushed to the missionary hospital at Zonkwa. It was there he was confirmed dead.

* * *

When I heard of his death, for a long time I did not believe it. My headmaster did not look like someone who could die. He looked too strong for death to even wrestle with him. It was after many days when I did not see him that I began to accept that my headmaster was indeed dead. When I remembered what he told us in our party, I wept. Metaphorically, he had told us we were having our last supper with him. But his metaphor in a very tragic way turned literal the following day in a manner none of us, including my headmaster could ever have imagined. What was said as a comic metaphor had turned into a literal tragedy, plunging my life and, I believe, the lives of many of my classmates into a nightmare we may never wake up from. It was like saying someone was a snake only for the person to turn into one before your very eyes.

For days on end, I wondered what was the meaning of life. For days on end, I wept for my headmaster.